The Iraqi Christ

by

Hassan Blasim

Translated by Jonathan Wright

Special Thanks

The author would like to thank the Iraqi writer and translator Adnan al-Mubarak for reviewing and editing most of the stories in the Arabic-language version of this book, and also to pay special thanks to his wonderful and creative friend, Ahmad al-Nawas, who discussed all the stories in the collection patiently and made many important and helpful observations. The author would also thank all the other friends who have offered support: Shadan Ahmad, Adel Abidin, Ahmad Awad, Marita Sandt and Paula Huhtanen.

First published in Great Britain in 2013 by Comma Press
www.commapress.co.uk

A CIP catalogue record of this book is available from the British Library.

ISBN 1905583524
ISBN-13 978-1905583522

The publisher gratefully acknowledges the support of Arts Council England.
In association with Literature Northwest.

Set in Bembo 11/13 by David Eckersall
Printed and bound in England by Berforts Information Press Ltd.

Contents

The Song of the Goats

PEOPLE WERE WAITING in queues to tell their stories. The police intervened to marshall the crowd and the main street opposite the radio station was closed to traffic. Pickpockets and itinerant cigarette vendors circulated among them. People were terrified a terrorist would infiltrate the crowd and turn all these stories into a pulp of flesh and fire.

Memory Radio had been set up after the fall of the dictator. From the start, the radio station had adopted a documentary approach to programming, without news bulletins or songs, just documentary reports and programmes that delved into the country's past. The station had become famous after announcing that it was going to record a new programme entitled *Their Stories in Their Own Voices*. Crowds gathered at the broadcasting centre from across the country. The idea was simple: to select the best stories and record them as narrated by the people involved but without mentioning their real names; then the listeners would choose the top three stories, which would win valuable prizes.

I succeeded in filling out the application form but made it inside the radio station only with great difficulty. More than once an argument broke out because of the crush. Old and young, adolescents, civil servants, students and unemployed people, all came to tell their stories. We waited in the rain for more than four hours. Some of us were subdued, others were bragging about their stories. I saw one man with no arms and a beard that almost reached his waist. He was deep in thought, like a decrepit Greek statue. I noticed the anxiety of the handsome young man who was with him. From a communist who was tortured in the seventies in the Baath Party's prisons, I heard that the man with the beard had a story that was tipped to win, but that he himself had not come to win. He was just a madman, but his companion, one of his relatives, coveted the prize. The man with the beard was a teacher who went to the police one day to report on a neighbour who was trading in antiquities stolen from the National Museum. The police thanked him for his cooperation. The teacher, his conscience relieved, went back to his school. The police submitted a report to the Ministry of Defence that the teacher's house was an al Qaeda hideout. The police were in partnership with the antiquities smuggler. The Ministry of Defence sent the report to the US Army, who bombed the teacher's house by helicopter. His wife, his four children and his elderly mother were killed. The teacher escaped with his life but he suffered brain damage and lost his arms.

I personally had more than twenty stories teeming in my memory about my long years of captivity in Iran. I was confident that at least one of them would really be the clincher in the competition.

They took in the first batch of contestants and then announced to the crowds left behind us that they had stopped accepting applications for the day. There were more than seventy of us that went in. They had us sit down in a large hall similar to a university cafeteria. A man in a smart suit then told us we were first going to listen to two stories to understand the format of the programme. He also spoke about legal aspects of the contracts we would have to sign with the radio station.

The lights gradually dimmed and the hall fell silent, as if it were a cinema. Most of the contestants lit up cigarettes and we were soon enveloped in a thick cloud of smoke. We started listening to a story by a young woman, whose voice reached us clearly from the four corners of the hall. She told how her husband, a policeman, was held by an Islamist group for a long time and how, during the sectarian killings, the killers sent his body back decomposed and decapitated. When the lights came back on, chaos broke out. Everyone was talking at the same time, like a swarm of wasps. Many of them ridiculed the woman's story and claimed they had stories that were stranger, crueller and more crazy. I caught sight of an old woman close to ninety waving her hand in derision and muttering, 'That's a story!? If I told my story to a rock, it would break its heart.'

The man in the smart suit came back on and urged the contestants to calm down. In simple words he explained that the best stories did not mean the most frightening or the saddest, what mattered was authenticity and the style of narration. He said the stories should not necessarily be about war and killing. I was upset by what he said, and I noticed that most of the contestants paid no attention. A man the size of an elephant whispered in my ear, 'It's bullshit what that bullshitter says. A story's a story, whether it's beautiful or bullshit.'

The lights went down again and we started listening to the second story:

'They found her feeding me shit. A whole week she was mixing it with the rice, the mashed potatoes and the soup. I was a sallow child, three years old. My father threatened to divorce her but she took no notice. Her heart was hardened forever. She never forgave me for what I did and I will never forget how cruel she was. By the time she died of cancer of the womb, the storms of life had carried me far away. I escaped from the country some time after the barrel incident, abject, defeated, paralysed by fear. On the night I said goodbye to my father, he walked with me to the graveyard. We read the first chapter of the Quran over my uncle's grave. We embraced and he slipped a bundle of cash into my hand. I kissed his hand and disappeared.

'We were living in a poor part of Kirkuk. The neighbourhood didn't have mains drainage. People would have septic tanks dug in their gardens for three dinars. Nozad the Kurdish vegetable seller was the only person in the neighbourhood who specialized in digging those tanks. When Nozad died his son Mustafa took on the work. They found Nozad burned to a cinder in his shop after a fire broke out one night. No one knows what Nozad was doing that night. Some people claim he was smoking hashish. My father didn't believe that. For all kinds of disasters his favourite proverb was 'Everything we do in this ephemeral world is written, preordained.' So in my childhood I believed that 'our life' was tucked away somewhere in school books or in the shop where they sold newspapers. My father wanted to save my childhood with all the goodwill and love he possessed. He was gracious towards others and towards life in a way that still puzzles me today. He was like a saint in a human slaughterhouse. Disaster would strike us pretty much every other year. But my father didn't want to believe that fate could bring such a mysterious curse. Perhaps he attributed it to destiny. We were liable to assault from every direction – from the unknown, from reality, from God, from people, and even the dead would come back to torment us. My father tried to bury my crime through various means, or at least erase it from my mother's memory. But he failed. In the end he gave in. He left the task to the ravages of time, in the hope that this would efface the disaster.

'I may have been the youngest murderer in the world: a murderer who remembered nothing of his crime. For me at least it was no more than a story, just a story to entertain people at any moment. What I noticed was that everyone would write, intone or sing the story of my crime as they fancied. At the time, my father wasn't working in the pickle business. He was a tank driver and the war was in its first year.

My mother was nagging my father for a third child but he refused because of the war, which terrified him. We were comfortably off. Every month my father would send enough money to cover food, clothing and the rent on the house. My mother would spend her time either asleep or visiting my aunt, with whom she'd talk all day about the price of fabric and the waywardness of men.

'In the summer, my mother went off into a dream world. She didn't listen, or talk, or even look. The midday heat would wipe her out. At noon she would take a bath and then sleep naked in her room like a dead houri[1]. When night fell she would recover some of her vitality, as if she had come out of a coma. She would watch her favourite soap opera and news programmes in which the president awarded medals for bravery to heroic soldiers, thinking that perhaps my father might appear among them.

'At noon one day, my mother dozed off with her arms and legs splayed open under the ceiling fan. My brother and I – he was a year younger than me – slipped off into the courtyard. There was nothing out there but a solitary fig tree and the cover of the septic tank. I remember my mother used to cry under the fig tree whenever one of our relatives died or some disaster struck us. The mouth of the tank was covered with an old kitchen tray held down by a large stone. We, my brother and I, had trouble moving the stone. Then we started throwing pebbles into the tank. It was our favourite game. Umm Alaa, our neighbour, used to make us paper boats that we would sail on the surface of the pool of shit.

'They say I pushed my brother into the tank and ran off to the roof of the house to hide in the chicken coop. When I grew up, I asked them, "Might he have fallen in, and I run away out of fear?" They said, "You confessed yourself." Perhaps they questioned me like the dictator's police. I don't remember anything. But they would tell their stories about it

1. Houri – one of the beautiful virgins of the Quranic paradise.

as if they were describing the plot of a film they'd enjoyed. All the neighbours took part in the rescue attempt. They couldn't find the truck that used to come once a month to empty out the septic tanks in the neighbourhood. They used everything they could find to get the shit out of the tank: pots and pans, a large bucket and other vessels. It was an arduous and disgusting task, like torture in slow motion. It was the height of summer and the foul odours added to the horror and the shock. Before the sun went down, they brought him out – a dead child shrouded in shit.

'My father was late coming back from the front. My uncle wrote him a letter and then took care of arrangements for the burial of my brother. We buried him in the children's cemetery on the hill. It may have been the most beautiful cemetery in the world. In the spring, wild flowers of every colour and variety would grow there. From a distance, the graveyard looked like the crown of an enormous, coloured tree: a cemetery whose powerful fragrance spread for miles around. A week later our neighbour Umm Alaa opened the door and saw my mother. The intensity of the grief had driven her to distraction. She had put shit in a small bowl, and was mixing it into my food very slowly with a plastic spoon, then filling my mouth with it as she wept.

'My father sent me to live with my uncle and I became a refugee of sorts. I would visit our house as a guest every Friday, escorted by my aunt to keep an eye on my mother. I felt like a ball that people kicked around. That's how I spent six years, trying to understand what was happening around me. I had to learn what their feelings and their words meant, all the while wearing a chain of thorns around my neck. It was like crawling across a bed of nails. The septic tank was the bane of my childhood. On more than one occasion I heard how life apparently advances, moves on, sets sail or, at worst, crawls slowly forward. My life, on the other hand, simply exploded like a firecracker in the sky of God, a small flare in His mighty firmament of bombardment. I spent the remaining years of my childhood and adolescence watching everyone carefully, like a sniper hidden in the darkness. Watching and shooting. Against the horrors of my life I unleashed other nightmares, imaginary ones. I invented mental images of my mother and others being tortured, and in my school book I drew pictures of enormous trucks crushing the heads of children. I still remember the picture of the president printed on the cover of our exercise books. He was in military uniform, smiling, and under his picture were written the words: "The pen can shoot bullets as deadly as the rifle".

'There was a cart that brought kerosene, drawn by a donkey. It came through the lanes in the neighbourhood in winter. The children would follow behind, waiting for the donkey's awesome penis to grow erect. I used to shut my eyes and imagine the donkey's penis, gross and black, going into my mother's right ear and coming out of the left. She would scream for help because of the pain.

'A year before the war ended my father lost his left leg and his testicles. This forced my mother to take me back. My father decided to go back to the trade practised by his father and his forefathers: making pickles. They say my grandfather was the most famous pickle seller in the city of Najaf. The king himself visited him three times. I went back home and acted as my father's dogsbody and obedient servant. I was happy, because my father was a miracle of goodness. Despite everything he had suffered in his life he remained faithful to his inner self, which had somehow not been warped by the pain. He had an artificial leg fitted and his capacity for love seemed to grow. He pampered my mother and showered her with gifts – golden necklaces, rings and lingerie embroidered with flowers.

'My father tiled the courtyard and made a concrete cover for the septic tank. He left some space for the fig tree but it died from the brine he used in the pickles. My mother wept beneath it for the last time when I was sixteen. The government in Baghdad had built a road for the highway and removed the old cemetery. Her father's grave had been there. For a long time we were sad about the loss of my grandfather's bones.

'The courtyard was full of plastic barrels for pickling, piles of sacks full of cucumbers, eggplants, green and red peppers, cabbages and cauliflowers, bags of salt, sugar and spices, bottles of vinegar and tins of molasses. There were also large cooking pots which were always full of boiling water, to which we would add spices, then all the vegetables one by one. My father wasn't as proficient as his father, let alone his grandfather. He started trying out new methods. He had spent a large part of his life in tanks and had forgotten many of the family recipes for making pickles. The tank had cost him his balls, his leg *and* the trade of his forefathers.

'I would sit opposite my mother for hours, cutting up eggplants or stuffing cucumbers with garlic or celery. Her tongue was as poisonous as a viper. The summer no longer bothered her. She had turned into a fat cow, burned by the sun, with a loose tongue, and smoked to excess. Noxious weeds had sprouted in her heart. People took pity on her, with words as poisonous as hers. "Poor woman," they said. "An impotent husband and no children, just the bird of ill omen." The bird, that was me, and I showed all the signs of ill omen. My father was busy all the time with the accounts and dealing with the shops in the market and moving barrels in the old pick-up. After sunset he would collapse from fatigue. He would have dinner, pray and tell us about his pickle problems, then take off his artificial leg and go to bed to tickle his grey-haired wife with his fingers.

'When the war over Kuwait broke out, I was meant to join the army. My father and my uncle sat down to discuss the question of my military service. My uncle had never seen the horrors of the front in the Iran War. He was working in the security department in the city centre. My father made up his mind: he would not give me up to die.

How can I let them kill my only son? My uncle argued with him, trying to explain how it would affect him in his branch of security if his nephew avoided serving the flag ("Do you want them to execute us all – us *and* the women?"). My father stuck to his position. My uncle threatened to arrest me in person if I didn't join the army, but my father threw him out of the house. "Listen," he said, "it's true I'm a peaceful man, but this is my son, a piece of my flesh. If you persist in this, I'll slit your throat." My uncle had been drunk that night and raging like a bull. He left shouting further insults. My father stood up, performed his prayers and quickly calmed down. "God save me from the accursed devil," he said. "He's my brother. It was just drunken talk. I know him. He has a good heart."

'I was a prisoner in the house for three months. The streets were full of military police and all the security agencies. My father decided I shouldn't work by day in case the neighbours noticed me. At night I would slip out into the yard like a thief, with a lantern in my hand. I would sit next to the sacks of eggplants, cucumbers and peppers, busy with my work and thinking about my life. I would mix arak[2] with water in an empty milk can so as not to get caught by my father, then get drunk and snack on the many varieties of pickle this tank driver had to offer. The alcohol would flow in my blood and I would crawl like a baby towards the septic tank, press my ear against the concrete cover and listen. I could hear him laughing. I would shut my eyes and imagine the feel of his bare shoulder. His skin was hot from all the playing and exertion. I no longer remembered his face. My mother had the only photograph of him and she wouldn't let anyone else go near it. She hid it in the wardrobe. She put the picture in a small wooden box decorated with a peacock.

'At the crack of dawn my father would get up. He would usually find me asleep in my place. He would put his hand on my forehead and I would wake up to the touch of

2. 'Arak' – a traditional, anise-flavoured distilled spirit.

his hand. "Go inside, son. Perform your prayers. May God prosper you." He was well aware I was drinking arak, but religion to him didn't mean the words of any prophet, any holy law or prohibitions. Religion meant love of virtue, as he would put it, to anyone with whom he was discussing questions of Islamic law. I will never forget the day he broke down in tears at the football ground. He frightened the children and I was embarrassed and disturbed that he was crying. The Baath Party members had executed three young Kurds close to the football pitch. They tied them to wooden stakes and shot them dead in full view of the local people. Before they did it, they announced over loudspeakers, "These people are traitors and terrorists who do not deserve to eat from the bounty of this land, or drink its water or breathe its air." As usual, the Baathists took the bodies and left the stakes in place to remind everyone of what had happened. My father had come to the square to take me to the cinema. He was crazy about Indian films. When he saw that one goal was missing an upright he realised we had taken the stakes to make the goals. Traces of blood had dried on the wood. My father broke down when one of the children said, "We're still missing one goalpost. Maybe they'll execute another one and we can have the stake."

'One summer evening we were invaded again. My uncle knocked frantically on the door. My mother was counting money and putting it in an empty tomato paste jar. My father and I were playing chess. He could beat me easily, but first he enjoyed giving me the pleasure of taking his pawns. He would sacrifice them and his other pieces without taking anything in return, keeping only his king and queen. Then he would start to destroy my pieces with his black queen until he had me in checkmate.

'My father went out to the yard to greet my uncle. My mother threw on her shawl and followed. They all stood near the septic tank in anxious discussion, but in low voices. I watched them from behind the window pane. I was still dizzy from drinking the day before. I was waiting for night to come to get drunk again. My mother rushed to fetch something from under the stairs. My father and my uncle worked together to empty a barrel full of pickled cauliflower. My mother came back with a hammer and a nail. My father laid the barrel flat on the ground and started to punch holes in it at random with the nail. He didn't have his artificial leg on. He was hopping around the barrel on one leg as if he were playing or dancing. My uncle parked the pick-up outside the front door and loaded it with the barrels of pickles. Then my father came into the living room sweating.

'"Listen, son," he said, "there's no time. Your uncle has information that the police and the party are going to search all the houses from dawn. Your uncle has loyal friends in the village of Awran. Stay there a few days till things calm down." I climbed into the empty barrel and my mother closed the lid tight. My father and my uncle lifted me on to the pick-up.

'My father was right. They were brothers after all, and they could read each others' minds. My uncle drove through the streets like a madman to save my life. He managed to reach the outskirts of the city safely but all the roads to the provincial towns and villages had military checkpoints. His only option was to take the back roads. He chose a road through the wheat fields to the east of the city. Maybe in his panic he mistook the road. Even the city children knew the chain of rugged and rocky hills that lay beyond the wheat fields. Maybe images of the people tortured in his department had unhinged his brain. Maybe he imagined his colleagues dissolving him in tanks of sulphuric acid and the headline *Security Officer Helps Nephew Escape in Pickle Barrel*. As he drove through the wheat fields, he was barely in control of the steering wheel. The bumps were about to break my ribs and only dust kicked up by the truck crept in through the holes in the barrel. The barrel stank like the dead cats on the neighbourhood rubbish dump. Did my uncle pull out fingernails, gouge out people's eyes and singe their skin with branding irons in the vaults of the Security Department? Maybe it was the souls of his victims that drove him into the ravine, maybe it was my own evil soul, or maybe the soul that preordained everything that is ephemeral and mysterious in this transitory world.

'Seven barrels lay in the darkness at the bottom of the cliff like sleeping animals. The pick-up had overturned after my uncle tried to take a second rocky bend in the hill. The barrels rolled down into the ravine with the truck. I spent the night unconscious inside the barrel. In the first hours of morning the rays of sunlight pierced the holes in the barrel, like lifelines extended to a drowning man. My mouth was full of blood and my hands were trembling. I was in pain and frightened. I started to observe the rays of the sun as they criss-crossed confusingly in the barrel. I wanted to escape the chaos that had played havoc with my consciousness. I felt as if I had smoked a ton of marijuana: a fish coming to its senses in a sardine tin, a dead worm in an abandoned well, a putrid foetus with crushed bones in a womb the shape of a barrel. Then my mind fixed on another image: my brother sinking to the bottom of the septic tank and me diving after him.

'The bleating sounded faint at first, as though a choir was practising. One goat started and then another joined in, then all the goats together, as if they had found the right key. The rays of the sun moved and fell right in my eye. I pissed in my pants inside that barrel, appalled at the cruelty of the world to which I was returning. The goatherd called out to his flock and one of the goats butted the barrel.'

The Hole

1

I WAS STUFFING the last pieces of chocolate into the bag. I had already filled my pockets with them. I took some bottles of water from the storeroom. I had enough tinned salmon – so I hid the remaining tins under the pile of toilet paper. Then, just as I was heading for the door, three masked gunmen broke in. I opened fire and one of them fell to the ground. I ran out the back door into the street, but the other two started to chase me. I jumped over the fence of the local football field and ran towards the park. When I reached the far end of the park, down by the side of the Natural History Museum, I fell into a hole.

'Listen, don't be frightened.'

His hoarse voice scared me.

'Who are you?' I asked him, paralysed by fear.

'Are you in pain?'

'No.'

'That's normal. It's part of the chain.'

The darkness receded when I lit a candle.

'Take a deep breath! Don't worry!'

He gave an unpleasant laugh, full of arrogance and disdain.

His face was dark and rough, like a loaf of barley bread. A decrepit old man. His torso was naked. He was sitting on a small bench, with a dirty sheet on his thighs. Next to him there were some sacks and some old junk. If he hadn't moved his head like a cartoon character, he would have looked like an ordinary beggar. He was tilting his head left and right like a tortoise in some legend.

'Who are you? Did I fall down a hole?'

'Yes, of course you fell. I live here.'

'Do you have any water?'

'The water's cut off. It'll come back soon. I have some marijuana.'

'Marijuana? Are you with the government or the opposition?'

'I'm with your mother's cunt.'

'Please! Is the place safe?'

He lit a joint and offered it to me. I took a drag and examined him. He looked suspicious. He smoked the rest of the joint and tuned a radio beside him to a station that was playing a song in a strange language. It sounded like some African religious beat.

'Are you foreign?'

'Can't you tell by my accent? I'm speaking your language, man! But you can't speak my language because I was in the hole before you. But you'll speak the language of the next person who falls in.'

'Ah, man. I hate the way you talk.'

He looked away, leant his tortoise-like neck forward and lit another candle. I could see the place more clearly now. There was a dead body. I examined it by the candlelight, a bitter taste in my mouth. It was the body of a soldier and there was an old rifle nearby. His legs were lacerated, possibly by some sharp piece of shrapnel. He looked like a soldier from ancient times.

'It's true, it's a Russian soldier.'

He read my thoughts and on his face there was an artificial smile.

'And what was he doing in our country? Was he working at the embassy?'

'He fell in the forest during the winter war between Russia and Finland.'

'You really are mad.'

'Listen, I don't have time for the likes of you. I wanted to be polite with you, but now you're starting to get on my nerves. I'm in a shitty mood today.'

I began to examine the hole. It was like a well. Its walls were of damp mud but the pores in the mud gave off a sharp, acrid smell. Maybe the smell of flowers! I lifted up the candle to try to see how deep the hole was. At the mouth, the lights in the park were visible.

'Do you believe in God?' he asked me in his disgusting voice.

'We're always in His care. Pray to Him, man, to spare us the disasters of life.'

He rounded his hands into the shape of a megaphone and started to shout hysterically: 'O Lord of Miracles, Almighty One, Omniscient One, God, Great One, send down a giraffe and a monkey as long as it's 180 centimetres tall! Make something other than a human fall in the hole! Make a dry tree fall in the hole! Throw us four snakes so we can make a rope out of them!'

As if the craziness of this tortoise-like old man was what I needed! I humoured him with his sarcastic prayer and said that if another man fell down the hole it would be easy to get out of it, because it wasn't deep.

'You're right, and here's a third man!' he said, pointing at the Russian soldier.

'But he's dead.'

'Dead here, but not in another hole.'

The old man suddenly pulled out a knife. I watched him warily, in case he attacked me. He crawled on his knees towards the body of the soldier and started cutting out chunks of flesh and eating it. He paid no attention to me, as if I didn't exist.

2

That night I had picked up my revolver before heading out to the shop. I'd closed the place down months before, when the killing and looting started to spread across the capital. I would drop by the shop now and then when it was hard to get food or water from any of the shops near our house. The economy had quickly collapsed and things had grown even worse due to the strikes. There were signs of an uprising and chaos spread in the wake of the government's resignation. The first protests began in the capital, and, within a few days, panic and violence swept the country. Bands of people occupied all the government buildings. They formed interim committees and attempted to govern. However things suddenly turned sour again. People said that it was businessmen who backed the organised gangs that managed to take control of the northern part of the country. The rich and the supporters of the fugitive government were convinced that the new faith-based groups would come to power and impose their obscurantist ideology. That's what the spokesman for the northern region said, and he also threatened that the region would secede. The extremists in the faith-based groups took no interest in speeches by politicians or revolutionaries. They were working silently behind the scenes, and in one shock assault they seized control of the country's nuclear missile base. 'Mankind has led us into ruination so let's go back to the wisdom of the Creator.' That was their motto.

As for the army, it fought on several fronts. In the country's main port, soldiers with machine guns killed more than fifty people who were trying to rob the main bank. People started to confront the army, which they began to see as the enemy of change. There was plenty of weaponry. Our southern neighbours were said to have given weapons to civilians. In the capital some sensible people called for calm and for a way out of the storm that was sweeping the country.

The army surrounded the missile base and began negotiating with the extremist leader, who was living among armed tribes in another country. He was a colonel who had been expelled from the army because of his extremist ideas. It was also said that he had a slogan tattooed on his forehead: *Purge the Earth of Devils*.

The old man chewed the meat and went back to his place as if he'd just finished eating a sandwich. He wiped his mouth with a dirty towel, pulled out a book, and began to read. I took out a bar of chocolate and devoured it nervously. The old man was quite loathsome and disgusting.

He looked up from his book and said, 'Listen, I'll get straight to the point. I'm a djinni.' He put out his hand for me to shake.

I looked at him inquisitively.

What was it my grandfather had said in his last few weeks? He kept raving in front of the pomegranate tree (all he could do in this world was suck pomegranates and stare at the tree).

How I wanted to get up and kick the old man. I noticed he was looking at me spitefully and smiling in a way that suggested contempt. Then he said, 'You seem to be braver and less disgusting than this Russian. Listen, I'm not interested in you and the people who visit the hole. All I'm looking for in your stories is amusement. When you spend your life in this endless chain, the pleasure of playing is the only thing that keeps you going. Wretches like this Russian remind me of the absurdity of the game. The romance of fear transforms the chain into a gallows. As soon as our friend the Russian fell in the hole, it terrified him that I was in it. He aimed his rifle at my head. And when I told him I was a djinni, he almost went crazy. He had one bullet. If it didn't kill me, he would die of fright, and if he didn't fire it he would remain hostage to his own paranoia.'

'Very well, and what happened?'

'Ha! I told him I knew all the secrets of his life, and to

make him more frightened I said I knew Nikolai, his aunt's youngest son. The soldier was disturbed when he heard the name. I talked about how he and Nikolai raped a girl in his village. He broke down and fired a bullet at my head. It's a silly chain, full of your human stories. Would you believe sayings such as this?' He read from his book: '"We are merely exotic shadows in this world." Trite talk, isn't it? Life is beautiful, my friend. Enjoy it and don't worry. I used to teach poetry in Baghdad. I think it's going to rain. One day we might know one of the secrets or how to get out. There's no difference here. What matters is the music of the chain.'

I shouted, 'You're eating a corpse, you disgusting old man!'

'Ha! You'll eat me too, and they'll eat you or use you as material for their batteries or for drinking.'

I punched him in the face and shouted again, 'If you weren't an old man, I'd smash your skull in, you bastard!'

He paid no attention to what I said. All he said was that there was no need for me to be upset, because he would leave the hole soon and I would fall into another hole from another time. He said his book would stay with me. It's a book full of hallucinations. It had detailed explanations of the secret energy extracted from insects to create additional organs to reinforce the liver, the pancreas, the heart and all the body's other organs.

3

Before leaving the hole, the old man told me he was from Baghdad and had lived in the time of the Abbasid Caliphate. He had been a teacher, a writer and an inventor. He suggested to the caliph that they light the city streets with lanterns. He had already supervised the lighting of the mosques and was now busy on his plan to expand the house lighting system by more contemporary methods. The Baghdad thieves were upset by his lanterns, and one day they chased after him after dawn prayers. Close to his home the lantern man tripped on his cloak and fell down the hole.

One of the things this Baghdadi told me was that everyone who visits the hole soon learns how to find out about events of the past, the present and the future, and that the inventors of the game had based it on a series of experiments they had conducted to understand coincidence. There were rumours that they couldn't control the game, which rolls ceaselessly on and on through the curves of time. He also said: 'Anyone who's looking for a way out of here also has to develop the art of playing, otherwise they'll remain a ghost like me, happy with the game… Ha, ha, ha. I'm fed up with trying to decipher symbols. There are two opponents in every game. Each one has his own private code. It's a bloody fight, repetitive and disgusting. The rest is memory, which they can't erase easily. In your day, experiments with memory were in their infancy. The scientists went on working for more than a century and a half after those first attempts – the purpose of which was to discover the memory centres in rats' brains. It turned out that the rats remembered what they learned even if their brains had been completely destroyed in the laboratory. Those would be amazing experiments if they were applied to humans. Is memory a winning card in this game that we play so seriously till it's all over, or should we merely have fun? Everyone that falls down here becomes a meal or a source to satisfy the instincts, or energy for other systems. We who…. damn, who are we? No one knows!'

The old man died and left me really helpless. Day had broken and snowflakes fell from the mouth of the hole. The Russian's body looked ghostly. I wanted to reach back to other times I might have lived in, the traces of which are scattered to places I previously thought imaginary. My consciousness was moving like a rollercoaster at a funfair. I watched the snowflakes swirling. The vision of the soldier had disappeared. My eyes were open and my mind was asleep. I may have been sleeping for hundreds of years. I imagined a dead cell. Am I really just in my mind or in every cell in my body? A strong smell of flowers filled the hole. I closed my eyes but then a young girl fell into the hole. She was carrying on her back an electronic bag tied around her chest with many straps, and to her thighs were tied metallic phosphorous clusters. In her hand she was holding something that looked like an electronic gauge.

'Who are you?' she asked me, panting. There were wounds disfiguring her pretty face.

'I'm a djinni. What happened to you?'

I felt as if my voice went back to ancient times.

'A blood analysis robot was chasing me,' she said.

She was sucking her finger, which was swollen like a mushroom.

'That's normal,' I said apathetically, then crawled towards the corpse of the old man.

The Fifth Floor Window

THEY WERE BOTH in their forties. They had colon cancer, while I had lung cancer. We were in the Medical City hospital in central Baghdad. The day before, they had taken Hajj Saber away. Poor guy. He died and escaped his torment. The cleaning woman came and changed the sheets on his bed. Salwan and I watched her as she arranged the bed carefully. She went through his little cupboard. She took out some towels and a bag of oranges his daughter Fatma had brought him the day before he died. The cleaning lady offered them to us. Salwan told her he wouldn't eat a dead man's oranges. Then he asked her irritably about the doctor and whether he would come by the ward any time soon.

'There isn't a single doctor available,' she answered, severe as usual. 'They're all in the emergency department. Haven't you seen the massacre from the window of your palace?'

Salwan had his very own rocking chair that he'd brought from home. He would put it close to the window and watch the courtyard outside the emergency department day and night. We were on the fifth floor. The courtyard never rested. Ambulances and cars would rush in and out like crazy. Sometimes carts would come, drawn by donkeys or horses, loaded with mangled bodies. It was hard to tell the dead from the living. It was a bleak year. Civil war. Infiltrators from abroad. Secret agents from all over the world. Adventurers. They were all making their way together down the river of hell that was Baghdad.

The doctors checked us with their white coats spattered with blood. The hospital was vast, with hundreds of patients lying in bed after bed. Salwan accused the doctors of negligence in the way they cared for the patients. They told him they couldn't even handle the emergency department because there weren't enough paramedics there. It was an exceptional situation. The country was being torn apart. But Salwan wasn't convinced. He held them responsible for the declining health of his fellow colon cancer victim – this was a retired pilot in a nearby bed who wouldn't stop groaning. On several occasions he had begged them to end his life. Salwan was frightened of his colon because it would soon get to the same stage as the pilot's, with the same excruciating pain. We were stuck between the pilot's groans and the bloody scenes outside the window. It was closed. We couldn't hear the screams of the injured and the lamentations of the bereaved in the courtyard of the emergency department. All we could hear were the pilot's groans, which sounded like cemetery music composed to accompany the drama we could see through the window.

Salwan's psychological state was constantly deteriorating. He was speaking but he was deaf to what anyone else said. All he could hear was the Angel of Death shuffling towards him. I learned that he'd been a carpenter all his life. His wife was barren. In his late forties, he took a second wife who was young. She made him happy with a handsome boy. The two wives would visit him regularly. They would sit on the end of the bed like squabbling crows. Salwan shared his insults equally between them, all without understanding a word of what they said. He was drowning in the depths of despair, like the wreckage of a ship.

That day Salwan was extremely tense. He woke up at dawn. A batch of human offerings had arrived when the first ray of sunlight touched the world of man: someone had blown himself up in the mosque during dawn prayers. Salwan lit a cigarette and walked up and down the ward muttering to himself. The nurse came in and asked him to put out his cigarette. He kicked up a ruckus, cursed the doctors, the suicide bombers and the cancer, and repeatedly damned the pilot for moaning, which gave him insomnia, he said. He didn't put out his cigarette until his shouting had woken everyone up. I got out of bed and fetched the teapot from the kitchen. We sat down together near the window drinking tea with biscuits. There hadn't been many people praying. The courtyard fell pretty quiet, except for the rain that was pelting down. I wanted to soothe his fears but I couldn't get the words straight in my mouth. Meanwhile he went on insulting Saddam Hussein and in my turn I cursed the Occupation. He asked me about the scorpion tattoo on the back of my hand and I told him it was a relic of my adolescence. I was in this gang at the time and we got together one drunken night on a piece of wasteland and decided that each of us would get a scorpion tattoo and we would be the Scorpion Crew. Salwan smiled. Suddenly his bad mood lifted and he too started to share memories of scorpions. He said that in his childhood he lived in a village that was full of poisonous snakes and scorpions. He talked about a girl called Parveen, and how they went hunting scorpions together:

'"Come here, Parveen, there's a black scorpion here!"

'Parveen would steal an empty bottle of tomato paste that her mother used to fill with water and keep in the fridge. I would remove the laces from my father's old army boots that were stored under the stairs. We would meet at the corner of the lane and set off towards the distant wheat fields. We would fill the bottle with water from the streams in the valley and embark on our search for scorpions. They weren't hard to find, because we could easily tell the scorpions' holes by their small size. They were round and went into the ground at an angle, and at the edge of the hole there would always be the little pile of soil they had dug out. The procedure was this: we poured water from the bottle into the scorpion's hole and the hole would soon fill up. In fact, pissing on the hole was usually enough to bring out the scorpion. We would piss when the water ran out. There were two stages to catching the thing: knowing that it would suffocate if it stayed in the hole, the scorpion tried to get out, but realising we were there waiting for it, it would only stick its head out. So, first we would dig underneath the scorpion with a spoon and throw it far from its hole. The scorpion would be terrified by this sudden attack and would scuttle about in search of a safe place under a stone or in another hole but... no way! Stage Two was to corner it and goad it into its new home – the tomato paste bottle. And in this house it would see all kinds of horrors and wonders. We'd cover the mouth with a plastic bag and tie it up with my father's boot laces.

'"Parveen, found one!"

'"Argh, it's yellow again!"

'We were looking for a black one because they were rare, and we could have fun watching a battle between a black one and a yellow one.'

Salwan walked as far as the pilot's bed and then came back, then stared into my eyes for several moments.

'The government executed Parveen's father for collaborating with the Kurdish peshmerga!'

'Do you have any gum?' I said. I noticed his nervous fingers.

He shook his head and returned to his bed. Then he pulled his blanket over him. I sat there thinking about my childhood, then about the situation with my wife and children. The operation would be in a week. They were going to cut out part of my lung. I didn't know if I would survive. How I longed to go back to reading! There was nowhere I longed to be more than the university campus. I was preparing a master's on fantasy literature. I was interested in why the country's literature did not include this distinctive genre. I had this great passion for studying and writing, which they explained in my household through the story of the umbilical cord. When I was born, and at my father's request, my elder sister buried my umbilical cord in the courtyard of her primary school. My father attributed my brother Adel's academic failure to the fact that my mother buried his umbilical cord in the garden of our house. I used to tease Adel saying, 'Instead of becoming a botanist or a farmer, you turned out unemployed.'

'We'll never know,' Adel replied. 'I've heard you say a thousand times this world is contradictory and mysterious, and there may be some connection between the garden and the bad luck that dogs me!'

Then he would give a laugh and swear that my father had told all his relatives and neighbours and colleagues at work the story about burying the umbilical cord.

The doctor visited the ward later that afternoon. He was a cheerful young man and performed a miracle when he drew a smile out of Salwan. He patted him on the shoulder and promised him that the specialist would be coming soon. After that, Salwan went back to looking out of the window. I heard him muttering to himself once more. The pilot's groans started to grow louder again, begging childishly for someone to spare him the pain of continuing to live. Salwan lost his temper. He started insulting and making fun of the pilot, and then accusing him: 'How many people did you kill with your warplanes? See how lucky you are! Hidden away in hospital when they're assassinating your colleagues, slaughtering them one by one.'

Salwan was right. But he wasn't right to add to the pilot's torment. After the fall of Baghdad an organised campaign to assassinate pilots had started. They said Iranian intelligence was taking revenge on them for their raids during the Iran-Iraq war. The nurse came in to help the pilot and warned Salwan to behave himself. Salwan and the pilot had been in the ward the longest. When I arrived they were close friends, chatting and joking all the time. But as soon as the pilot's health collapsed, Salwan went crazy because the pilot's colon reminded him what was also in store for him.

That night Salwan sat close to the pilot's bed. They were whispering to each other. I was lying in bed reading *Palomar* by Italo Calvino. Mr Palomar was thinking, 'But how can you look at something and set your own ego aside? Whose eyes are doing the looking? As a rule, you think of the ego as one who is peering out of your own eyes as if leaning on a windowsill, looking at the world stretching out before him in all its immensity.' Salwan gave me a strange look then went back to whispering with his friend. He stood up and put his hand on the pilot's shoulder, as though trying to reassure him about something. After a while he moved the wheelchair close to the bed and asked me to help him sit the pilot in it. After that, Salwan pushed the wheelchair to the window. I went back to bed and watched him. I thought the pilot wanted to share the view. Salwan came over to my bed. He wanted to say something but he stepped back and spun around, sunk in thought. I was suspicious of his behaviour. His face was pale and he looked like death was about to grab him.

I think that a view like the one from the window has an irresistible power. It pulls one towards committing a crime. The mind can also be addicted to, and live off, the carrion of fear. Perhaps my mind was just a hyena looking for carrion. I had turned to stone in my bed, like the Baghdad statues, pale, exhausted by fountains spitting blood. Salwan pushed the pilot's chair back a little. He picked up a chair and with three violent blows in succession he smashed the window pane. He brought the pilot's chair up to the window frame, then went back to his bed and dived inside it.

The pilot climbed up onto the window sill with difficulty. He was screaming with pain and the broken glass was shredding the palms of his hands. With a great effort he pushed his body through the window and fell forwards into that courtyard of bloody battle.

The Iraqi Christ

WE WERE MEANT to camp in an old girls' school and some of the soldiers decided the best place to spend the night was the school's air-raid shelter. Daniel the Christian picked up his blanket and other bedding and headed out into the open courtyard.

'Of course, Chewgum Christ is crazy,' remarked one of the soldiers, a man as tall as a palm tree, his mouth stuffed with dry bread.

'Perhaps he doesn't want to sleep with us Muslims,' suggested another soldier.

The young men were monkeys. They didn't know the truth about Daniel. They were too busy masturbating on the benches in the classrooms where the girls used to sit. Just one missile and they would shortly be charred pricks. In absurd wars such as this one, Daniel's gift was a lifesaver. We had been together in the Kuwait War and if it hadn't been for his amazing powers we wouldn't have survived. Aside from his gloomy nature, Daniel could hardly be considered ordinary flesh and blood. He was a force of nature.

I spread out my blanket close to him and lay on my back, like him, staring into space.

'Go to sleep, Ali, my friend. Go to sleep. There's no sign tonight. Go to sleep,' he said to me, and started snoring straight away.

Daniel was always chewing gum. The soldiers baptized him Chewgum Christ. I often imagined that Daniel's chewing was like an energy source, recharging the battery that powered the screen in his brain. His life's dream was to work in the radar unit. He had completed secondary school and volunteered to join the air force, but his application was rejected, maybe because his father had been a prominent communist in the seventies. He loved radar the way other men love women or football. He collected pictures of radar systems and talked about signals and frequencies as though he was talking about a romp in the hay with some girlfriend. During the last war, I remember him saying, 'Ali, humans are the best radar receivers, compared with other animals. You just need to practise making your spirit leave your body and then bring it back, like exhaling and inhaling.' He had tattooed on his right arm the radar equation:

$$P_r = \frac{P_t G_t A_r \sigma F^4}{(4\pi)^2 R_t^2 R_r^2}$$

After Daniel's hopes of joining the air force were dashed, he volunteered for the medical corps. But he did not give up his passion for radar, and anyone who knew him would not have been surprised by this obsession, because Chewgum Christ was himself the strangest radar in the world. I remember those terrifying nights during the war over Kuwait. The soldiers, as frightened as ducklings, would follow him wherever he went. The coalition planes would be bombing our trenches and we wouldn't be able to fire a single shot back. We felt we were fighting some ultimate, almighty force. All we could do was dig more trenches and scamper from place to place like rats. In the end we camped near the desert. All we had left was our faith in God and the powers of Daniel the Christian. One night we were eating in the trench with the other soldiers when Daniel started complaining of a stomach ache. The soldiers stopped eating, picked up their weapons and prepared to stand, all of them looking at Daniel's mouth.

'I want to lie down in the shade of the large water tank,' Christ said finally.

The soldiers joined him as he left the trench, jostling to keep close to him as if he were a shield against missiles. They sat around him in the shade. Just thirty-five minutes later three bombs fell on the trench. It wasn't the only time. Christ's premonitions saved many soldiers. In Daniel's company the war played out like the plot of a cartoon film. In the blink of an eye, reality lost cohesion. It fell apart and you started to hallucinate. What could one make, for example, of the way a constant itching in Daniel's crotch foretold that an American helicopter would crash on the headquarters building? Is it credible that three successive sneezes from Daniel could foretell a devastating rocket attack? They fired them at us from the sea. We soldiers were like sheep, fighting comic book wars.

I heard many rumours that reports on Christ had been submitted to the Supreme Command. But the chaos of those days and the defeat of our army, which was crushed like flies, prevented the authorities paying any attention. There were many stories about the president's interest in magicians, the occult and people with prodigious powers. They claim it was at his suggestion that so many books on parapsychology were unexpectedly translated in Iraq in the eighties, because he had heard that the advanced countries were developing telepathic techniques and using them for espionage. The president thought that science and the occult were one and the same, they just used different methods to reveal the same secrets. Christ was not boastful about his premonitory powers and did not consider them unusual. He used to tell stories from history about mankind's ability to foretell the future. I came to the conclusion that Daniel's melancholia made it impossible for him to take pleasure in the talent he possessed. Even his interest in radar did not bring him pleasure. His ideas about happiness were mysterious. I understood from him that he was frightened by some inner gloom. He thought his talent was just another sign of how impotent and insignificant we are in this mysterious world. He told me that at an early age he read a story by an Iraqi writer whose personality was simultaneously sarcastic and fearful. The hero in the story was swallowed by a shark after a fierce battle in the imaginary river of time. The hero sits trapped in the darkness there and thinks alone: 'How can I reconcile my private life with my awareness that a world is collapsing in front of my eyes?'[3] 'That's a question that has weighed on my life. It has kept me awake like an open wound,' said Christ.

When we woke up the next day the American forces had reached the outskirts of Baghdad. A few hours later they brought down the statue of the dictator. It was a surreal shock. We put on civilian clothes and went back to our families. It was just another war of the blind in which no one in our squadron fired a single shot. After it was all over, I met Daniel several times. He had gone back to live with his elderly mother. When chaos broke out in the country, I visited him in their house in Baghdad. I wanted to speak to him about going back to the army. He said he had hated the dictator but he would not contribute to an army under the auspices of the occupier. After that I didn't meet him again. I myself returned to the army, and Daniel went back to looking after his mother. He had two sisters who had migrated to Canada years before and his other relatives had left the country one by one, driven away by wars and the madness of sectarian fanaticism. Of his large family, only his mother remained. I found out that Daniel spent most of his time at home reading novels and encyclopaedias, following the news and caring for his mother, who had lost her hearing, her sight and her memory. Old age isolated her from the world. The old woman was incontinent. Christ would change her nappies every few hours. His mother's death would sever the

3. As Ingmar Bergman once asked in an interview.

thread that tied him to the place. He didn't plan to emigrate. In a long letter, his older sister implored him to leave the country, but Christ was as stubborn as his mother. Both of them rejected the devil's temptation – to abandon their lost paradise.

After mass one Sunday, Christ took his mother to a local restaurant famous for its kebabs. He liked the cleanliness of the place and the way it set aside seats for children. The restaurant had changed greatly. He couldn't remember the last time he had been there. Christ chose an empty table in the corner and helped his mother to sit down. The waiter's good humour cheered him up. The man would mix up the names of the dishes with the names of daily instruments of slaughter. The customers laughed and loved him. He would call out orders such as 'One explosive, mind-blowing, gut-wrenching kebab. One fragmentation stew. Two ballistic rice and beans.'

Christ asked for one and a half orders of kebab with hot peppers, a glass of ayran[4] and a cold juice. The waiter came back with the order and made a joke about inquisitive people. Christ smiled politely. He picked up his mother's fingers gently and placed them down to feel the hot kebabs and the grilled tomatoes. Then he put them back in place on the edge of the table. He picked up a tasty morsel and pressed it into her mouth, smiling at her with extraordinary, selfless love.

A young man asked if he could sit down at Christ's table. Stocky in build and with a hard expression on his face, he was probably about twenty. He ordered a kebab with extra onions. He was actually quite handsome but was scratching his neck incessantly like someone with scabies. His eyes shifted from table to table. Daniel moved the plate of salad closer to his mother's fingers and left her to feel out the vegetables on the plate. He prepared another mouthful for her. The young man watched them stealthily. He seemed eccentric. He kept chewing his piece of meat and trying to swallow it, as tears

4. Ayran – a cold beverage of yoghurt mixed with iced water and sometimes salt.

streamed from his beautiful eyes. Daniel was wary of him. He leaned forward and asked if he could help. He repeated the question but the young man kept his eyes on his plate and did not seem to have heard Daniel. He kept chewing and his tears flowed. He took out a handkerchief, wiped away his tears and cleaned his nose. He looked around the restaurant, then stared into Christ's eyes. His features changed to reveal another face, as though he had taken off a mask. He grasped the flap of his jacket and pulled it aside like someone baring his chest.

'It's an explosive belt. One word from you and I'll blow myself up,' the young man said, with a threatening glance towards the old woman.

I was killed by friendly fire, myself. We were on a joint patrol with the American forces after the invasion. Someone opened fire on us from a house in the village. The Americans responded hysterically, thinking we had opened fire on them. I was shot three times in the head. I met Christ in our next world, and we were overjoyed. He told me how he was inexplicably drawn to that young man in the kebab restaurant. It wasn't just terror that had paralysed him, but also some mysterious desire for salvation. For some moments he stared into the young man's face. The man leaned towards him and asked him to stand up and go to the bathroom with him. At first he didn't budge from his place, as if turned to stone. Then he kissed his mother's head and stood up.

The young man led the way to the toilets. He closed the door and kept the tip of his finger on the button on the explosive belt. With his other hand he pulled a pistol out of his belt and pointed it at Daniel's head. The young man was practically hugging Christ by this point, wrapping his arms around him because the space was so tight. He summed up what he wanted – Daniel should wear the explosive belt in his place, in exchange for him saving the old woman's life.

The young man was in a hysterical state and could hardly control himself. He said there would be someone filming the explosion from outside the restaurant and that if he didn't blow himself up they would kill him. Daniel said nothing in response. They started to sweat. One of the customers tried to push the toilet door. The young man cleared his throat. Then he again promised Christ he would take the old woman safely out of the restaurant, but if Daniel didn't blow himself up he would kill her. Half a minute of silence passed, then he agreed with a nod of his head and stared blankly into the young man's eyes. The young man asked him to undo the belt and wrap it around his own waist. It was a difficult process because the room was so narrow. The young man withdrew cautiously, leaving Christ in the toilet with the explosive belt on. Then he rushed towards the old woman in the corner of the restaurant. He tapped her gently on the shoulder and took hold of her hand. She stood up and followed him like a child. The restaurant had started to fill up and the noise level was rising, as people laughed and the cutlery clattered like a sword fight.

Christ fell to his knees. He could hardly breathe and he pissed in his trousers. He opened the bathroom door and crawled into the restaurant. Someone met him at the door and ran back shouting, 'A suicide bomber, a suicide bomber!'

Amidst the panic, as men, women and children trampled on each other to escape, Christ saw that his mother's chair was empty and he pressed the button.

The Green Zone Rabbit

BEFORE THE EGG appeared, I would read a book about law or religion every night before going to sleep. Like my rabbit, I would be most active in the hours around dawn and sunset. Salsal, on the other hand, would stay up late at night and wake up at midday. And before he even got out of bed he would open his laptop and log on to Facebook to check the latest comments on the previous night's discussion, then eventually go and have a bath. After that he would go into the kitchen, turn on the radio and listen to the news while he fried an egg and made some coffee. He would carry his breakfast into the garden and sit at the table under the umbrella, eating and drinking and smoking as he watched me.

'Good morning, Hajjar. What news of the flowers?'

'It's been a hot year, so they won't grow strong,' I told him, as I pruned the rose bushes.

Salsal lit another cigarette and gave my rabbit an ironic smile. I never understood why he was annoyed by the rabbit. The old woman Umm Dala had brought it. She said she found it in the park. We decided to keep it while Umm Dala looked for its owner. The rabbit had been with us for a month and I had already spent two months with Salsal in this fancy villa in the north of the Green Zone. The villa was detached, surrounded by a high wall and with a gate fitted with a sophisticated electronic security system. We didn't know when zero hour would come. Salsal was a professional, whereas they called me duckling because this was my first operation.

Mr Salman would visit us once a week to check how we were and reassure us about things. Mr Salman would bring some bottles of booze and some hashish. He would always tell us a silly joke about politics and remind us how secret and important the operation was. This Salman was in league with Salsal and didn't reveal many secrets to me. Both of them made much of my weakness and lack of experience. I didn't pay them much attention. I was sunk in the bitterness of my life, and I wanted the world to be destroyed in one fell swoop.

Umm Dala would come two days a week. She would bring us cigarettes and clean the house. On one occasion Salsal harassed her. He touched her bottom while she was cooking dolma. She hit him on the nose with her spoon and made it bleed. Salsal laid off her and didn't speak to her after that. She was an energetic woman in her fifties with nine children. She claimed she hated men, saying they were despicable, selfish pricks. Her husband had worked in the national electricity company, but he fell from the top of a lamp post and died. He was a drunkard and she used to call him the arak gerbil.

I built the rabbit a hutch in the corner of the garden and took good care of him. I know rabbits are sensitive creatures and need to be kept clean and well-fed. I read about that when I was at secondary school. I developed a passion for reading when I was thirteen. In the beginning I read classical Arabic poetry and lots of stories translated from the Russian. But I soon grew bored. Our neighbour worked in the Ministry of Agriculture and one day I was playing with his son Salam on the roof of their house, when we came across a large wooden trunk up there with assorted junk piled up on top of it. Salam shared a secret with me. The trunk was crammed with books about crops and irrigation methods and countless encyclopaedias about plants and insects. Under the books there were lots of sex magazines with pictures of Turkish actresses. Salam gave me a magazine but I also took a book about the various types of palm tree that grow in the country. I didn't need Salam after that. I would sneak from our house to the roof of theirs to visit the library in the trunk. I would take one book and one magazine and put back the ones I had borrowed. After that I fell in love with books about animals and plants and would hunt down every new book that reached the bookshops, until I was forced to join the army.

The pleasure I found in reading books was disconcerting, however. I felt anxious about every new piece of information. I would latch onto one particular detail and start looking for references and other versions of it in other writings. I remembered, for example, that for quite some time I tracked down the subject of kissing. I read and read and felt dizzy with the subject, as if I had eaten some psychotropic fruit. Experiments have shown that chimpanzees resort to kissing as a way to reduce tension, fatigue and fear among the group. It's been proven that female chimpanzees, when they feel that strangers have entered their territory, hurry to their mates, hug them and start kissing them. And after long research, I came across another kiss, a long tropical kiss. A kiss by a type of tropical fish that kiss each other for half an hour or more without any kind of break. My memory of those years of darkness under sanctions is of devouring books. The electricity would go off for up to twenty hours a day, especially after that series of U.S. air strikes on the presidential palaces. I would snuggle into bed at midnight and by the light of a candle I would stumble upon another species of kiss: by insects called reduvius, though they don't actually kiss each other. These only like the mouths of sleeping humans. They crawl across the face till they reach the corner of the mouth, where they settle down and start kissing. When they kiss they secrete poison in microscopic drops, and if the person sleeping is in good health and sleeping normally, he'll wake up with a poisonous kiss on his mouth the size of four large raindrops put together.

I ran away from military service. I couldn't endure the system of humiliation there. At night I worked in a bakery. I had to support my mother and my five brothers. I lost the urge to read. For me the world became like an incomprehensible mythical animal. A year after I ran away, the regime was overthrown and I was free of my fear of punishment for my earlier desertion. The new government abolished conscription. When the cycle of violence and the sectarian decapitations began, I planned to escape the country and go to Europe, but then they massacred two of my remaining brothers. They were coming back from work in a local factory that made women's shoes. The taxi driver handed them over at a fake checkpoint. The Allahu Akbar militias took them away to an undisclosed location. They drilled lots of holes in their bodies with an electric drill and then cut off their heads. We found their bodies in a rubbish dump on the edge of the city.

I was completely devastated and I left home. I couldn't bear to see the horror on the faces of my mother and brothers. I felt lost and no longer knew what I still wanted from this life. I took a room in a dirty hotel until my uncle came to visit me and suggested I work with his sect. To exact revenge.

The summer days were long and tedious. It's true that the villa was comfortable, with a swimming pool and a sauna. But to me it seemed like a palatial mirage. Salsal took a room on the second floor, while I was content with a cover and a pillow on the sofa in the middle of the large sitting room where the bookcase stood. I wanted to keep an eye on the garden and the outer gate of the villa, in case anything unexpected happened. I was stunned by the size of the bookcase in the sitting room. It had many volumes on religion and on local and international law. Along the shelves, animals made of teak had been arranged in shapes and poses reminiscent of African totems. The animals also separated the religious books from the law books. As soon as it fell dark, I would grab a bite to eat and go and surrender myself to the sofa, reminisce a little about the events of my life, then take out a book and read distractedly. The world in my head was like a spider's web that made a faint hum, the hum of a life about to expire, of breaths held. Delicate, horrible wings flapping for the last time.

I found the egg three days before Mr Salman's last visit. One day I woke up at dawn as usual. I fetched some clean water and food and went to inspect my friend the rabbit. I opened his hutch and he hopped out into the garden. There was an egg in the hutch. I picked it up and examined it, trying to understand the absurdity of it. It was too small to be a chicken's egg. I was anxious so I went straight to Salsal's room. I woke him up and told him about it. Salsal took hold of the egg and stared at it for a while, then laughed sneeringly.

'Hajjar, you'd better not be pulling my leg,' he said, pointing his finger towards my eye.

'What do you mean? It wasn't me who laid the egg!' I said firmly.

Salsal rubbed his eyes, then suddenly jumped out of bed like a madman, firing curses at me. We headed to the villa gate and checked the security system. We inspected the walls and searched the garden and all the rooms. There were no signs of anything unusual. But an egg in a rabbit hutch! Our only option was to think that someone was playing tricks on us, sneaking into the villa and putting the egg next to the rabbit.

'Perhaps it's a silly stunt by that whore Umm Dala. Damn you and your rabbit,' said Salsal, but then went quiet.

Both of us knew that Umm Dala was sick and hadn't come to visit us for the past week. We were doubly afraid because we didn't have any guns in the house. We weren't allowed to have guns until the day of the mission. They were worried about random searches because the Green Zone was a government area and most of the politicians lived there. We were living in the villa on the pretence that we were bodyguards to a member of parliament. Salsal threw a fit and asked me to slaughter the rabbit, but I refused and told him the rabbit had nothing to do with what had happened.

'Wasn't it your bloody rabbit that laid the egg?' he said angrily as he went up to his room.

I made some coffee and sat in the garden watching the rabbit, which was eating its own droppings. They say the droppings contain vitamin B produced by tiny organisms in its intestines. After a while Salsal came back carrying his laptop. He was mumbling to himself and cursing Mr Salman from time to time. He looked at his Facebook page and said we had to be on alert 24-7. He asked me to spend the night in his room on the second floor because it was good for monitoring the gate and the walls of the villa.

We turned off all the lights, sat in Salsal's room and every now and then took turns in making a tour of inspection around the villa.

Two nights passed without anything suspicious. The villa was quiet, sunk in silence and calm. While I was staying in Salsal's room I learned he was registered with Facebook under the pseudonym War and Peace and had posted a charcoal drawing of Tolstoy as his profile picture. He had more than a thousand Facebook friends, most of them writers, journalists and intellectuals. He would discuss their ideas and pose as an intelligent admirer of other Facebook people. He expressed his opinions and his analysis of the violence in the country with modesty and wisdom. He even tried it on with me, rambling on about the character of the Deputy Minister of Culture. He told me how cultured and humane and uniquely intelligent he was. At the time I wasn't interested in talking about the deputy minister. I told him that people who work in our line of business ought to keep their distance from too much internet chat. He gave me his sneering professional look and said, 'You look after your egg-laying rabbit, Hajjar.'

When Mr Salman finally visited us, Salsal exploded in anger in front of him, and told him about the rabbit's egg. Mr

Salman ridiculed our story and dismissed our suspicions of Umm Dala. He assured us the woman was honest and had worked with them for years. But Salsal accused him of betrayal and they began to argue, while I sat watching them. From their argument I gathered that in the world of sectarian and political assassinations, people were often betrayed because of greater interests. In many cases the parties in power would hand over hired killers to each other for free, as part of wider deals over political positions or to cover up some large-scale corruption. But Mr Salman denied all Salsal's accusations. He asked us to calm down, because the assassination of the target would take place in two days. We sat down in the kitchen and Salman explained the plan to us in detail. Then he took two revolvers with silencers out of his bag and said we would be paid right after the operation and that we would then be moved to somewhere else on the edge of the capital.

'A rabbit's egg. Ha, duckling. You're a real joker now,' Salman whispered to me before he left.

On the last night I stayed up late with Salsal. I was worried about the rabbit, because it looked like Umm Dala would be on a long holiday. The rabbit would die of hunger and thirst. Salsal was busy with Facebook as usual. I stayed close to the window, watching the garden. He said he was having a discussion with the Deputy Minister of Culture on sectarian violence and its roots. I gathered from Salsal that this minister had been a novelist in Saddam Hussein's time and had written three novels about Sufism. One day he and his wife were at a party at the home of a wealthy architect overlooking the Tigris. His wife was attractive, stunningly so, and cultured like her husband. She had a particular interest in old Islamic manuscripts. The Director of Security, a relative of the president, was a guest at the party. After the party was over, the security chief gave his surveillance section orders to read our friend's novels. A few days later they threw him in jail on charges of incitement against the State and the Party. The Director of Security bargained with the novelist's wife in exchange for her husband's freedom. When she rejected his demands, the security chief had one of his men rape the woman in front of her husband. After that the woman moved to France and disappeared. They released the novelist in the middle of the nineties and he went off to look for his wife in France, but could find no trace of her. When the dictator's regime fell, he went home and was appointed Deputy Minister of Culture. The story of the novelist's life was like the plot of a Bollywood film, but I was surprised how many details of the man's life Salsal knew. I felt that he admired the man's personality and sophistication. I asked him what sect the man was. He ignored my question. Then I tried to draw him out on the identity of our target, but Salsal replied that a novice duckling like me wasn't allowed to know such things. My only task was to drive the car and it was Salsal who would fire the shot with his silenced revolver.

The next morning we were waiting in front of the car park in the city centre. The target was meant to arrive in a red Toyota Crown and as soon as the car went into the car park Salsal would get out of our car, follow him inside on foot and shoot him. Then we would drive off to our new place on the edge of the capital. That's why I had brought the rabbit along with me and put it in the boot of the car.

Salsal received a text on his mobile and his face turned pale. We shouldn't have had to wait for the target more than ten minutes. I asked him if all was well. He shouted out a curse and slapped his thigh. I was worried. After some hesitation he held out his mobile phone and showed me a picture of a rabbit sitting on an egg. It was a silly Photoshop job. 'Do you know who sent the picture?' he asked.

I shook my head.

'The Deputy Minister of Culture,' he said.

'What!!?'

'The deputy's the target, Hajjar.'

I got out of the car, my blood boiling at Salsal's stupidity and all the craziness of this pathetic operation. More than a quarter of an hour passed and the target didn't appear. I told Salsal I was pulling out of the operation. He got out of the car too and asked me to be patient and wait a while longer, because both of us were in danger. He got back in the car and tried to contact Salman. I walked to a shop nearby to buy a packet of cigarettes. My heart was pounding like crazy from the anger. As soon as I reached the shop the car blew up behind me and caught fire, burning the rabbit and Salsal to cinders.

A Wolf

FEAR ALSO HAS a smell, as you know.

The man smelled of smoked fish as he spoke, spraying saliva from his mouth.

'That was last winter. I was coming back from one of my routine jaunts around the city centre. Jaunts intended to "pick up a living", as we say in the home country. I was gathering what I could from various, out-of-the-way bars: casual conversation, a fuck, a free beer, a joint, anarchic talk about political matters, an argument with another drunk, or a chance to annoy others on the pretext of being drunk, just for fun. The important thing was that the day should include a human touch, however small. You know. And on the day the wolf appeared, I met a strange young woman. An owl of ill omen, as we would say. Do you believe there are faces that bring bad luck? There are faces you meet that are like the symbols in dreams. You're an artist and your imagination makes it easy for you to understand what I mean, doesn't it? You artists are farmers tilling the fields of dreams. Do you like that? Yes, I believe in dreams more than I believe in God. Dreams get into you and leave, then come back with new fruit, but God is just a vast desert. Imagine there's an Indian painter in Delhi working on some subject that's also taking shape in the dream of a man who's asleep in Texas. Okay, fuck that. But would you agree with me that all art comes together in this way? Perhaps love and unhappiness too. If, for example, a poet wrote about loneliness in Finland, then his poem could be the dream of someone asleep in some other part of the world. If there was a special search engine for dreams, like Google, all dreamers would find their dreams in works of art. The dreamer would put a word, or several words, from his dream into the Dream Search Engine, and thousands of results would appear. The more the search is narrowed down, the closer he gets to his dream and eventually he finds out it's a painting or a piece of music or a sentence in a play. He would also find out which country his dream was in. Yes, you know. Maybe life... okay, fuck that.

'The young woman had a surprising face. It looked like the needle of an electric sewing machine had pricked it for many hours. Her complexion was peppered with dozens of little holes. She told me she was Spanish. Then, five minutes later, she told me her mother was Egyptian and her father Finnish. She only knew three words of Arabic, all of them related to sexual organs or blasphemous phrases including the word "shit". The whore drank three glasses of beer on my account and went to wait in a dark corner. What do you think she's waiting for? Definitely another prick who'll spend more on her. I lost twenty euros in the slot machine. I felt exhausted and hungry. Then I waved at the woman with the ill-omened face, a sarcastic theatrical wave, and before leaving, as if addressing vast throngs, I shouted: "Long live life!"

'On the way home, I couldn't get the woman's face out of my mind. I had the impression I had met her in some street market in the country. I don't know why, but I imagined her sitting wrapped in a black cloak selling green and red peppers. I'm certain that three or four signs of bad luck had conspired to put me in this mess. But anyway, listen, you won't believe what happened next. As usual, as soon as I got back to my flat, I took off all my clothes. I was on my way to the bathroom when I saw the thing running towards me from the sitting room. I jumped into the bathroom and slammed the door behind me. I was like someone who'd seen the Angel of Death. It was a wolf. A wolf, I swear. But you'll say that maybe it was a dog. After looking through the keyhole several times, I spotted it again and I knew very well what it was. I was really shaking. There was a terrifying silence for some minutes. After looking through the keyhole several times, I could see it – I was sure it was a wolf. I could hear it panting, then I saw it sniffing my trousers and underpants at the front door. After that it sat down and started to stare sadly at the bathroom door.

'A wolf in the city centre, in a block of flats, and in *my* bloody flat! I sat on the toilet seat and began to think: no one but me had a key to this flat, I live on the fourth floor, and even if we assume, okay, that it could fly and had come in through the balcony, the door between the sitting room and the balcony was always closed. I pissed without noticing I was doing it. I sat there as if paralysed, naked on the toilet seat with a wolf in my flat. How absurd! I began to blame and curse myself. Why did I strip off like a whore whenever I came into the flat? If I'd had my mobile with me, I would have called the police and it would all be over. What kind of shitbag am I? An unemployed drunk, cruising the bars to pick up a living. And from whom? From wrecks no less rotten than me; people from under whose feet the new world of glitter has pulled the carpet, like, for example, that fat woman in her late thirties looking for a casual fuck with an immigrant refugee who doesn't have a screw left that's not loose. We're the ones who don't have delicious tight arses. We just have arseholes to shit from. But fuck that.

'Even the woman I met that day, the one with the face punctured with needle holes, didn't take up my invitation. She moved to another table and waited for better rubbish to come along. If she'd accepted my invitation to fuck and come back to the flat with me, she would have run off and called the police or the neighbours. Perhaps the wolf would have eaten her. What wolf? Impossible. There must be some mistake in the facts of this case, or some hallucination. I was speaking like this to my image in the mirror.

'I looked through the keyhole again. It was crouched in the same place. There were only a few hours left till morning. I thought that tomorrow someone would be worried I was missing. Of course it was a ridiculous idea, and my only aim was to give myself some false consolation. Because I've been living alone for years, and I only know freaks that haunt the most secluded bars, and they're like me – loners who scrape together a livelihood where they can, or else slope back to their dirty beds to be consumed by sadness the long night through. The only ones who might knock on my door are the Jehovah's Witnesses, and they stopped coming a while back. Perhaps they've had enough of my constant mockery of their Lord. There was a time when they would swamp me with their books and magazines. One thing I liked in those magazines was that desperate attempt to link the discoveries of science to the stories in the Bible. Two beautiful women from the Jehovah's Witnesses used to visit me regularly. My sick imagination made me welcome them warmly. I thought that establishing a serious relationship with them would lead to passionate lovemaking. Imagine. The two Jehovah's Witness women, naked in my bed. One of them sucking my cock and the other giving her clitoris to my tongue while reading a passage from the Bible. We used to talk about lots of things. The subject that interested me most was the fact that Jehovah's Witnesses don't believe in blood transfusions. I used to joke with them and say that blood is delicious and it's what vampires drink. I used to talk to them about the importance of blood.

'"The Director of the Bio-Ethics Centre at the University of Pennsylvania says in complete scientific coldness, 'The importance of blood in healthcare is comparable to the importance of oil in the transport sector. Just as billions of barrels of oil are extracted every year to satisfy the human demand for fuel, about ninety million units of blood are drawn from volunteers to save mankind. That vast amount of blood is equivalent to all the blood in the veins of eight million people.' Nonetheless, blood stocks seem to be insufficient. Just like oil. There are constant warnings about this shortage."

'This cocktail of scientific information or, to be more precise, pretentious waffle, was so that the Jehovah's Witnesses would know I really was an important person before I came to Finland and began to stagnate. I told them I was an expert on Hebrew and that I translated secret reports for the Ministry of Defence and the Intelligence Agency. To make my professional life sound more exciting, I added some adventures, detective book stuff. With them I would prattle on at length, making up stories and mixing serious talk with nonsense. I would pose questions too, and answer them myself while the women sat there like doves of peace. They would smile as if they had just arrived from heaven.

'"But what if a deadly plague broke out across the world and everyone needed new blood?" Before the older woman could guess the answer, I would say, like an expert explaining genetic science, "Without a doubt, a new global war would break out. But even so, there's no need to worry because, if a war for blood did break out, I think it would be a clean war in which they would ban the use of traditional weapons, or modern weapons, or even paring knives. So the war would be like a game of American Football and the soldiers would wear padded sports clothes. Of course there would be no point fighting a war in which blood flowed for no purpose, at a time when the world was in dire need of it, so there would be no toleration or mercy towards soldiers who used weapons of any kind. But what kind of war would that be? Fuck that. The aim of the fighting would be to capture as many of the enemy troops as possible. The troops would clash, and each side would try to capture the other's troops and then move them away in trucks that would wait in the rear lines. It would be the last war and it would come to an end when the last person gave blood. The trucks would take the captive soldiers to blood donation centres and the blood would then be distributed fairly among the population..."

'But we've strayed from the subject. Is my chatter making you dizzy? Fuck that. Okay. Anyway, there I was, talking to myself and shaking. "The wolf, my god, the wolf! Why doesn't it move from its place?" I wimpered. Why doesn't it at least go to the kitchen to look for something to eat? All it did while posted in front of the bathroom door was sniff my underwear, then stare at the door with murderous eyes. Of course, it was a shitty idea for me to leave the forest and come back to live in the city. Damn those blood-sucking mosquitoes. Did you know it's the female mosquitoes that feed on human blood, while the male drinks only the sap of plants and the nectar of flowers? I spent more than five months in the forest, catching fish every day in the nearby lake and in the evening translating an interesting book on the grammar of the Hebrew language. I was happy in my seclusion, with the gifts of the forest, oblivious to the world of humans. I would drink red wine, in moderation. But the disaster was that none of the creams with which I covered my face and body deterred the mosquito attacks. And how could I relax when a swarm of them was hovering over my head all day long like Christ's halo in those old paintings? At night the female ones got through the sheets like armoured vehicles and sucked my blood greedily. The landlord made fun of me when I told him about the mosquitoes. He said they must like me a lot. And finally my sufferings from the mosquitoes were topped by a severe stomach ache. The doctor told me it was just my irregular diet and I should eat more vegetables. He also said it would be best if I went back to the city and mixed with people. The stomach clearly suffers when you live in isolation. I also gathered from him that I had started to talk about myself in a peculiar way. In short, he believed I needed a psychiatrist. Okay. I'm a good listener most of the time and I appreciate advice. But I only stuck to the first half of the doctor's advice. I came back to the city and went back to mixing with the dregs of secluded bars. Without a drink, the world needs a bull-fighter. With a drink, the world is a farce that only needs more clowns. Fuck that.

'Inside the bathroom there was only the towel and piles of dirty socks and underwear. I was exhausted and cold. I checked that my guest was still in his place. I took a hot shower and went back to thinking about the matter. If I had any enemies, it might be logical to think that the supposed enemy had brought the wolf to my flat. But how would you take a wolf to another man's flat without help from someone who works in a zoo and without a special vehicle for carrying wolves? Perhaps it's a tame wolf, like a dog. Or maybe I've gone mad and I'm simply imagining all this. Could a sensible man believe what I'm telling you? Don't say you believe me, but it is, by Jehovah and all his witnesses and angels, a real wolf. Perhaps the doctor was right.

'I covered myself with the towel and fell into a deep sleep on top of the socks and underwear. When I woke up, I had a severe headache ploughing through my skull like an angry bulldozer. It might have been midday. The other mad thing that's hard to believe is that the wolf was still in its place. Shit. Doesn't it feel hungry, and why's it as still as the Sphinx? The idea of hunger seeped into my mind like a quicksilver snake. I panicked and let out a loud scream. Was I to stay trapped in the bathroom till I died of hunger, if the wolf didn't die of hunger first? Of course, wolves can put up with hunger better than humans. But I have the water in the bathroom, whereas the kitchen tap won't do him any good. But then he might die of thirst while I die of hunger. No, no. In the kitchen there's a pan of soup on the table. I don't know if he'd like last night's soup, and besides, there's bread on the table too if he wants it...

'I suddenly had a horrendous attack of hysteria and started pounding on the door and screaming for help. Every now and then I would check the reaction of the damned wolf through the hole. Where are the neighbours? Have they had wolves as well? No, no, I can't possibly die here in the bathroom. I thought it would be better to be eaten by the wolf than to die in this horrible way and not be eaten! I was looking in the mirror and going over my fears to myself. Perhaps I could wrestle with the wolf and make good my escape. Perhaps he would just wound me. And even if he bit an entire arm off that would be better than rotting to death in the bathroom. I splashed water on my face, brushed my teeth and examined my reflection for more than a quarter of an hour. I kicked the wall, raving and cursing. Then I had an idea: why not open the door, throw the towel at it and see how far I get? But, brave guy, what if the wolf pounces instantly and you can't escape? I did another round of shouting and banging on the walls, hammering on them with the shampoo bottles until they broke. Then I collapsed on top of the toilet seat again. I cupped my hands and drank water from the sink, then burst out crying. I threw myself on the cold tile floor and curled up like someone with a religious zeal to disappear from this world.

'Late on the second night, I decided to put an end to this nonsense. Either he ate me or I would eat him myself. I felt an amazing energy, driven by my thirst for revenge. I would tear apart this worthless, cowardly wolf. I would cut him up and roast his flesh, and his head too. Fuck that! I opened the bathroom door ever so slowly. The wolf jumped to its feet. I ran with all my strength and leapt towards it. The last thing I remember was when the wolf leapt towards me.

'It was a cold and frightening darkness. Solid darkness. The only thing that helped me in the emptiness was remembering what happened in those last moments, although the horror of having my body disappear paralyzed my attempt to be patient and to await the mercy of God in that darkness. What I had thought is that, when you die, no thread of memory survives, no awareness of the life you lived; quite the opposite of what happened in my case. Although death, as absolute nothingness, is no more than an assumption. I wanted to shout out to ask for help but I didn't know where my mouth was or even how I could shout. What was the mechanism or the motions I had to perform in order to shout? How could I work out where my foot was, or how could I find my hair to touch it? Was I dead? The problem with that darkness was not that you couldn't remember what it was like to perform some action or other. The trouble was that, in the sea of darkness, you lose the means to perform it. You remember how to look, for example, but you no longer have the tools that make it possible to look. At the same time, I felt that I still existed as a small point of consciousness somewhere in the world. I don't know how long this lasted. The small point expanded. The breathing, and a sense that my skin was somehow warm, began to come back, slowly at first but at a rate that gradually accelerated.

'Apparently I had hit my head on the edge of the small nightstand and lost consciousness. I bled a little. There wasn't any wolf in the flat. It had vanished as if into thin air. The flat door was closed and only the bathroom door was open. I put on a shirt and took my mobile phone from the pocket of my trousers, which lay on the floor close to where the wolf had been before it disappeared. Rather warily, I wandered around the rooms. There was no one at home but me. I sat down on the edge of the sofa and turned on the television. There was a repeat of the Oscars award ceremony. Brad Pitt had his arm round Angelina Jolie's waist and was talking about his chances of winning an award. I decided to go back to the forest and try to stand up to the mosquitoes, instead of seeing them as crocodiles. Fuck that. This is the last glass I'll drink with you. You really are a strange man – perhaps you're rather like me. You have a suspicious capacity for listening. I think you are... Okay. Perhaps another glass before I go. Fuck that. I didn't catch your name... I'm Salman.'

'Hassan Blasim, pleased to meet you.'

Crosswords

In memory of my friends:
Dawoud the engineer, 2003
Kouresh the poet and doctor, 2006
Bassem the sculptor and photographer, 2007

HE WAKES UP.

It's a mess of a morning.

He hears the words: 'For God's sake, I'm going to die of thirst!'

He sits on the edge of the bed. He feels a numbness in his limbs. He pours himself a glass of water. He looks around the ward in a daze. He sees a bird hitting the window pane. A plump nurse is giving an injection to a man with an arm missing.

'Aha! Cold water! Thank you,' says the policeman somewhere deep inside him...

My lifelong friend Marwan used to say, 'Across: mankind; down: the sea. The highest mountain peak in the world. A three-letter word. An unfamiliar reality.'

They published a picture of him smiling on the cover of the magazine!

It was a picture taken two years ago during the ceremony at which he received the prize for being the best crossword writer. The prize was funded by a billionaire member of parliament who came back to the country after the change in regime. They say the great passion he acquired for crosswords during his long exile was behind his decision to finance the prize. It was worth 15,000 dollars. The prize aroused much envy among certain journalists and writers who criticized it severely and at length. Marwan won it on merit; I think Marwan could be awarded the title 'Poet Laureate of Crosswords'.

I found some of his old crossword puzzles at the farm once. They contained strange expressions such as 'half a moon', 'a semi-mythical animal', 'a vertical tunnel', 'a poisonous grass', and 'a half-truth'.

In the olden days, when our eyes were like magnifying glasses, the moon was a giant that rose above the rooftops, and we wanted to break it with a stone. In those days Marwan and I were like a single spirit. One autumn evening we lit a fire in a barrel of rubbish and swore an oath to be forever loyal to each other. We played often, and invented our own secrets, built our own world out of the strangeness of the world around us. We watched the adults' wars on television and saw how the front ate up our elders. Our mothers baked bread in clay ovens and sat down in the sunset hour, afraid and with tears in their eyes. We would steal sweets from shops, climb trees and break our legs and arms. Life and death was a game of running, climbing and jumping, of watching, of secret dirty words, of sleep and nightmares.

I remember you both well. I felt like a third wheel when we all started secondary school. I was jealous of you!

Marwan and I would chase the coffins. We would wait for them to reach the turning off the main road. The war was in its fourth year by this point. The coffins were wrapped in the flag and tied firmly to the tops of cars that came from the front. We wanted to be like grown-ups who, when a coffin passed by, would stand and raise their hands solemnly and sadly. We would salute the dead like them. But when the death car turned a corner, we would race after it down the muddy lanes. The driver would have to slow down so that the coffin didn't fall off. Then the car would choose the door of a sleeping house, and stop in front of it. When the women of the house came out they would scream and throw themselves in the pools of mud and spatter their hair with it. We would hurry to tell our mothers whose house the death car had stopped outside. My mother would always reply, 'Go and wash your face,' or 'Go to Umm Ali next door and ask her if she has a little spice mixture to spare.' And in the evening my mother would go and mourn with the local women in the dead man's house, slapping her face and weeping.

Once I was sitting with Marwan waiting for a coffin to arrive. We were eating sunflower seeds. We had waited a long time and were about to give up hope and go back home disappointed. But then the death car loomed on the horizon. We ran after it like happy dogs and were betting on who could beat the car, when it finally stopped in front of Marwan's house. His mother came out screaming hysterically. She ripped her clothes and threw herself in the pool of mud. Bassem, who was standing next to me, stood stock still and stared in a trance. His big brother noticed him and pulled him into the house. I ran back home, into my mother's arms, crying in torment. 'Mummy, my friend Marwan's dad's died,' I sobbed. She said, 'Wash your face and go to the shop and fetch me half a kilo of onions.'

I heard what you wrote yesterday. How the first explosion shredded Marwan's face. The windows shattered and the cupboards fell on top of him. His mouth filled with blood. He spat out teeth and indistinctly heard the screams of his colleague, the editor of the New Woman section. The dust made it impossible to see. She crawled over the rubble screaming, 'I'm going to die… I'm going to die.' Then she fell silent suddenly and forever. Marwan bled a long time and only recovered consciousness in hospital.

Okay.

Marwan had cute and interesting ideas when we were kids. Once he asked me to help him collect time. We went down towards the valley, stretched out on our stomachs and proceeded to stare at a weed without moving for more than an hour. We were as silent as stone statues. It was Marwan's belief that if we stared at anything in nature for an hour we would store that hour in our brains. While other people lost time, we would collect it.

It was a double explosion. First they detonated a taxi in front of the magazine's offices. If it hadn't been for the concrete barriers the building would have collapsed. The second vehicle was a watermelon truck, packed with explosives. The first police patrol to arrive after the first explosion brought three policemen. The murderers waited for people to gather and then detonated the second vehicle. That killed twenty-five people. Two of the policemen were killed on the spot and their colleague caught fire and began running in every direction. Finally he staggered through the door of the magazine building and collapsed, a lifeless corpse.

In an old text of yours you say:

A pulp of blood and shit
a monster
a defiled planet
a god-viper
time spilled in that time.

When we were in secondary school we used to fuck a prostitute who would give us her customers' shoes. She loved us like a mother. She bought us lots of chocolate and laughed when she slept with us. Marwan used to steal spoons and knives from his house and offer them to her as presents. She was crazy about little knives and addicted to crossword puzzles. We called her 'the drunken boat' after the poem by

Rimbaud. Before the school year ended, we went on a school trip to explore the mountains. Marwan tried to bring 'the drunken boat' along with us, but the headmaster threatened to expel us from school. On top of a rock shaped like the head of an angry bull, overlooking the valley, we sat down to smoke and read the newspaper. The others went off to explore a cave where prehistoric man had once lived. It was small, like an animal's burrow, and full of spiders' webs, they told us later. I read the paper while Marwan smoked and then we would switch roles. It was a government newspaper and it was pathetic, from the political news on the front page to the back page devoted to the mysteries of the other world, as if our own world weren't strange and incoherent enough. It was on top of the bull's head that Marwan discovered his vocation. He solved the crossword puzzle in the newspaper in an instant. After that he got a notebook and pen out of his bag and set to work writing his own crossword. He smoked six cigarettes before he finished his first puzzle. It was made up of synonyms from nature. From the rock he stared up at the treetops and said, 'Writing crosswords is much easier than solving them.'

'Perhaps it's like the real world,' I said, blowing smoke and pretending to be a dreamy young man.

'What a philosopher,' he said sarcastically. Then he gave an absurd, euphoric yell that filled the valley.

That night he told you that 'the drunken boat' was his relative. Why did he hide this from you for so many years?

We were separated when we went to university. Marwan's family moved to another part of the city. He went to study agriculture, with dreams of ending up with a piece of land where he could plant pomegranate trees. I went to the faculty of mass communications. We would visit each other constantly, exchange ideas, laugh, smoke and drink a lot. We would also exchange gossip about 'the drunken boat'. We heard that some pimp had cut off her ear because she stole a ring from a customer who worked in State Security. She got her revenge on him three days later. He was lying asleep on his stomach so she sank a carving knife deep into his arse. She was given a jail sentence.

Marwan got married in his first year at university. It was passionate love at first sight. The fruit of his love with Salwa was two children, and the fruit came while they were still studying. When they graduated, Salwa stayed at home to look after the children and Marwan went looking for work. Things weren't easy for someone who had just graduated in agriculture. Meanwhile, I started to have articles published on historical esoterica, which I had been writing since I was a student. After I graduated, I began work straight away at the magazine, *Boutique*. We would vent our need to rebel by writing on ideological and social themes. I got in touch with a colleague who was working in the popular magazine *Puzzles* and told him that Marwan was skilled at writing crosswords and astrology columns. Marwan was angry with me for lying about the astrology but he had no options other than to work at the magazine. He started writing crosswords and even began swatting up on astrology.

He sent you a text message that read: Fire Sign – You're compatible with all the signs. Your blood group breathes disappointment and happiness. You stick your tongue in the woman's mouth in order to cool down. The fog that burns on the ceiling is the steam of sweat. You buy pins and coloured pictures from the shop. You pin them on your flesh when you receive a guest. The firewood comes to you throughout the night, wrapped in nightmares. When you wake up you have a bath on fire. You eat on fire. You read the newspapers on fire. You smoke a cigarette on fire. In the coffee cup you come across prophecies of fire. You laugh on fire. You have your lungs checked at the hospital, and they find a spring of errors that looks like a tumour. You dream of the final act: it goes out.

I bought a stuffed scorpion from the toyshop and went to visit Marwan in hospital. The doctor told me that Marwan's injuries weren't serious. They had extracted some fragments of window glass from his scalp and said he would be fine. Salwa, his wife, was anxious and frightened by Marwan's mental confusion. Like her, I asked the doctor various questions about Marwan's mysterious condition. The doctor asked me, 'If you'd gone through a terrorist explosion like that, would you come out laughing and joking?'

'Maybe!' I said, looking at his pointed nose.

He gave me a contemptuous look and took Marwan's wife to one side.

The doctor was wrong; Marwan wasn't just suffering from shock. The burnt policeman had got inside him and had taken control of his being. He would say he could hear the policeman's voice in his head, clear and sharp.

Aahh! Perhaps like my voice... you frame his sarcastic words and hang them on your living room wall.

War

Peace

God's arse

After coming out of hospital Marwan kept to himself at home and didn't want to meet any visitors. One day he contacted me and said he wanted to come visit. We bought a bottle of whiskey and went to my apartment. He told me he was reluctant to go to the policeman's house and find out who he was.

He soon got drunk and started shouting and cursing, addressing thin air, saying, 'Eat shit' and 'Shut up, pimp.'

Then he opened his eyes like an owl and threatened to

break off our friendship if I didn't believe everything he told me. I took the policeman's address from him and drove him home. Salwa was waiting for us at the window, downcast. Marwan hadn't told her what had happened to him. He was struggling to deal with the disaster himself and was on the verge of madness.

I knocked on the door and an attractive woman in the spring of her life came out. She was dressed in black and her eyes were swollen. Standing in the doorway, I saw a little girl playing with a rabbit the same size as her. I said I was a journalist and I wanted to write an article about the victims of the explosion at *Puzzles* magazine. She said her husband had been killed because of the ignorance that prevailed in this wretched country and she didn't want to speak to anyone. She shut the door. I made discrete enquiries about the young woman's circumstances at a nearby shop. The shopkeeper told me about her husband, the policeman, and how kind he had been and how much he had loved his family. The policeman used to say, 'God has blessed me with the three most beautiful women in the world – my mother, my daughter and my wife. I'm thankful to be alive, however tough it is in this country.'

In the three days Marwan spent in hospital, the policeman told him what had happened: 'On the patrol we were telling each other jokes, my colleagues and me. We heard the explosion and headed straight to the Puzzles building. My colleagues moved people away from the scene of the incident and I tried to put out the fire in a car in which a woman and her daughter were burning. Then the second explosion went off.

'My body caught fire. I started to run and scream, then I collapsed in the lobby. I found myself sitting on the ground, a few paces away from my own burning body! I had split in two: one a lifeless corpse, the other shivering from the cold. I ran down the corridors of the magazine building. I saw a woman crawling on her stomach and screaming, but she died before I could do anything. I saw you under the rubble, so I went inside you and I felt warm again. And here I am, smelling what you can smell, tasting what you taste, hearing what you hear, and aware of you as a living being, but I can't see anything. I'm in total darkness. Can you hear me?'

'Yes,' Marwan had said.

Okay, this is what you wrote down… tell me how you reacted to that.

Marwan was angry when I suggested he visit a man of religion. I was bewildered by what he told me and it had made me say stupid things. He told me I was mad and that I was still behaving like we were childhood soulmates. ('It was just a trivial, childish game, you idiot!' he yelled.) Then he started talking to me as calm as a madman: 'Do you understand me? Okay, he can share a bed with me, a grave, a window, a seat on the bus, but he's not going to share my body! That's too much, in fact it's complete madness! He grumbles and cries and tells me off as though I'm the thief and it's not him who's stolen my life.'

If Marwan went to sleep with only a thin blanket around him, the policeman would wake him up in the middle of the night and say, 'I'm cold, Mr Marwan, please!'

If Marwan drank whiskey, the other guy would complain, 'Please, Mr Marwan, that's wrong. You're burning your soul with that poison! Stop drinking!'

Or: 'Why don't you go to the toilet, Mr Marwan? The gas in your stomach is annoying.'

Why couldn't it have been the policeman who incited Marwan to swallow the razor blade?!

Marwan's eyes turned bloodshot from staying up late and drinking too much, and the others got used to his behaviour.

They treated him as a victim of the explosion. Just another madman. His nerves would flare up for the slightest reason. His colleagues at work didn't abandon him, and he went on devising crosswords, though he stopped writing the horoscopes. He was given a warning when he started writing very difficult crosswords, using words he found in the encyclopaedia or when he wrote, for example, '7 Across: a purple scorpion, 5 Down: a broken womb (six letters, inverted).'

'This meat tastes salty. What's that horrible smell? Don't you read the Quran? Why don't you pray? The water's hot in the shower.' Marwan started to take revenge, taking pleasure in tormenting the policeman. He would eat and drink and do things the policeman didn't like, like drink gallons of whiskey, which the policeman couldn't bear.

Marwan complained to you about the things that troubled him most. He hadn't gone near his wife's body, except once, three months ago. He had the impression that he was sleeping with her along with another man, and the policeman groaned and wailed like a crazed cat.

The policeman didn't submit to his fate readily. He also knew how much authority he had. Sometimes he would keep jabbering deliriously in Marwan's head until his skull throbbed. The last time Marwan told me about the policeman was while they had a truce.

The policeman wanted Marwan to visit his family. He told him some intimate details of his life so that Marwan would seem like an old friend. Yes, yes, yes. I'm not interested in all those details. When you write, you can choose the limits and call the rest our ignorance.

Marwan sat on the sofa and the policeman's wife brought him some tea, while his mother wiped her tears with the hem of her hijab. Marwan hugged the policeman's little girl as if she were the daughter of a late dear friend.

It was the same scene whenever he visited. He started buying presents for the family on instructions from the policeman, and Marwan even went to visit the policeman's grave with the family.

The policeman went into a deep silence when he heard his wife and mother weeping at his grave. He remained silent for several days. Marwan breathed a sigh of relief each time, assuming the policeman had disappeared.

He punched you on the nose when you were driving the car. I know… good… details… everything in this story is boring and disgusting.

Then one day I visited him at his magazine. He was taking swigs from a bottle of arak that he hid in the drawer of his desk and smoking furiously. I started talking about our problems working at *Boutique* and the state of the country, in the hope of calming his nerves. He stopped writing as I spoke.

When I stopped speaking, he stood up and asked if I'd go with him to visit the 'drunken boat' in prison.

I wasn't even sure she was still alive. I rang the department in charge of women's prisons from his office and asked after her. They told me she was a patient in the city's central hospital.

I was extremely uneasy all the way to the hospital. Marwan smoked a lot and rocked back and forth in his seat. He began pressing me to take good care of his family, his voice full of emotion.

I told him, 'What are you talking about? Marwan, what do you mean, "going to die"? Hey, you're like a cat with seven good lives left.'

He punched me on the nose. Then he lit me a cigarette

with his one and put it in my mouth. I had an urge to stop the car and give him a thorough beating.

The 'drunken boat' was lying in the intensive care ward. Just a skeleton. She'd been unconscious for a fortnight. We sat close to her on the edge of the bed. Marwan took a small knife shaped like a fish out of his trouser pocket and put it close to her pillow.

He held her hand and tears flowed down his cheeks.

And after that you came to visit me!

Yes, we bought a range of mezes, two bottles of arak and twenty cans of beer, and we drove to your farm.

I was so happy to see the two of you! Time had flown, you guys! We had a wild time that night raising a toast to our memories of secondary school. We put a table out, under the lemon tree and cracked open the drink. Marwan seemed cheerful and relaxed, without any obvious worries. He was laughing and joking, not to mention drinking frantically. Somebody brought up that boy at school called 'the Genius'. He was an eccentric student who memorised all the text books by heart within months. The teachers were convinced he was a genius, and they were shocked when he got poor grades in the end of year exams, barely enough to qualify to study in the oil institute. In his first year of college, he sneaked in at night and set fire to the lecture hall, then shot himself with a revolver. It was all a bit of a tragedy!

You told us at length about your days of isolation on your farm, where you wanted to be free to write a book on the history of decapitation in Mesopotamia.

The conversation eventually flagged and we started to slur our words. We were drunk and Marwan fell back into a deep silence. We got up to go into the house. Marwan asked me to recite whatever I could remember by Pessoa, his favourite writer.

I'm not me, I don't know anything,
I don't own anything, I'm not going anywhere,
I put my life to sleep
In the heart of what I don't know.

It was a wonderful summer's night. Three best friends from school reunited. I lay on the grass, looked up at the clear sky and began to imagine God as a mass of shadows. We heard Marwan's screams coming from the bathroom. We couldn't save him. He died in the pool of blood he had vomited.

You phoned me a week later and we went to an art exhibition in my car. We were going along the highway when, by mistake, I overtook a truck loaded with rocks.

Enough, God keep you.

What, you're tired!

I want to sleep a while.

Okay, let's sleep.

I hope that when I wake up I can't hear you any more and you're completely out of my life.

Me too, you fuck.

Dear Beto

I GOT RID of him. A few days ago, as I was roaming in the forest. But now I feel tired. I haven't slept for three nights. I can smell a wolf approaching!! Please, Beto, go to my aunt's place, take my stuff and look after all my memories.

You can't understand beauty without peace of mind and you can't get close to the truth without fear. Do you remember the guy who used to teach us smells? He used to make us dizzy with his wild philosophical speculations. He used to call himself the faithful companion of knowledge. He was proud of you and greatly admired you, so much so that I thought Professor Azmeh was in love with you. Those days of studying are still engraved in my memory, before we had to hit the mean streets and our dreams went up in smoke. Do you remember when that fourth year student brought in a cat one weekend? It was a farce. Everyone smelled its rear-end and there was such an uproar. Those were really romantic days. If our friend Sancho had been here, he would have said in his flippant tone: 'The world is swimming in a sea of shit.' They say he's become a philosopher. Three epic tracts – long theses exploring the rationale for living with humans.

You too, Beto, you used to turn everything into philosophy. At the time, I thought you would get involved in the world of thinkers yourself. But you're lazy and you've always said that language is deceptive. I still remember every word you told me when we were going round the back lanes looking for a safe place. I still remember the beautiful morning we spent on that river bank. The sun was shining like a giant pomegranate. We went up to a woman in her late forties who was crying and swearing at everything around her. She looked at us with tears in her eyes and started telling us her sorrows. She said she had failed in love, and failed in hatred, too! We chased her and then went back under the bridge. You licked my neck, then gave a sigh and sounds started to come out of you, quiet and frightened. (When you suddenly lose everything and snap like a bone, a door in your soul flickers open and closed as quick as an eyelash, a door that opens into the hidden self, the self that lies beyond pain. But not all humans are cruel enough to grasp the secrets of such a magic door, because humans are soon broken, like brittle bones. They fall into the abyss of pain and become blind.) Perhaps we're like them too. I don't know, Beto. I just want to disappear I'm so lonely.

We jumped into the lake together. He was drunk as usual. I dived underneath him, grabbed the end of his trouser leg and dragged him under until he stopped breathing.

Marko had brought me on a trip with some artist friends to the outskirts of a beautiful town in the centre of Finland. At first I didn't believe he would ever free the two of us from the cruel seclusion he had imposed on us. For a year and a half I had been living in the prison of his sad life. He had torn my soul with his loneliness and opened old wounds with his rude behaviour. He violated my body and destroyed the fragile peace of mind where I hoped I might take refuge in this land of snow and ice.

There was a large isolated house in the forest, a house that was far from electricity, the internet and gas cookers. When they cooked, he and his friends made a wood fire in an old stove. They chopped the wood themselves. At night they lit a fire, drank and sang and chatted. There was a lake where they went fishing. It's a real life there. They write poems, draw and plan theatre and film projects. Yes, the place was like a little paradise and as my owner put it, the ideal place to die. If we could look inside his mind, we'd find him imagining a grave in the middle of the forest, in a place where the sound of the forest stirs the vegetation into forms of great beauty. Indeed! Because the sound of insects and birds, the wind playing in the branches and the crackle of burning wood in the fire pit all combined to create a symphony of sounds; perhaps the voice of God reaches us in that sound, directly, without the mediation of prophets. God exists in the forest. God is the forest. But the burial ground must also be in the forest, so that the trees can draw their life from our decomposing bodies. I'm still a romantic, Beto, but yes, now I've fallen into the trap of hatred.

There were four of them and I was the fifth. They were trying to draw up a schedule for the next day, if there was anything worth doing communally, such as fishing, riding bicycles through the forest, or walking to the lake and coming home at sunset. There was a tall young man called Miko Lahm, a hunter who had come with his dog to catch birds. I spent some time with his dog. He was full of himself, like most hunting dogs. He was one of those creatures in whom the delusion of intelligence casts a shadow over their thoughts. He was proud of his muscles and of his ability to track down and retrieve wounded birds, and his master, Miko, was a real expert in all kinds of hunting and fishing, including rabbits; he cooked all kinds of meat in a way that everyone said was amazingly professional. Although most of the friends were vegetarians, and others only ate fish. So you might say that Miko Lahm was hunting for himself. Sometimes he was happy that I would share the meat with him. Of course he didn't let his own dog eat the meat he hunted. He gave him dog food from cans.

Paulina spent the time lying in the sun on an orange towel. She was reading a book about plants. Timo, her partner, was sitting nearby, just smoking and gazing at the trees. He would dig into the soil with his feet, then examine the soil carefully as if it were a human corpse, then smoke another joint and stare at the sky. When he'd put out his fourth joint he would go back to the trees, then start the cycle again by scratching at the soil once more, like a dog but this time more slowly. He would light another joint, and never once speak to Paulina. The staring and smoking and all that deliberate idleness continued for four hours, broken only when he stood up and fetched a bottle of beer from the house. My master, Marko, would draw occasionally, while Miko Lahm played with his dog. At first sight I must have looked like I was the happiest of them all, because the slow pace of life in the forest really cheered me up. I had almost forgotten my recent sufferings with Marko. Time there passes at an amazingly glacial pace. You would laugh, Beto, and show your terrible teeth, if I told you that the first task I undertook there was to practise emptying out my mind and spreading its contents out in the sun to dry. I wanted to be alone with myself with a mind that wasn't soaked in doubts. I would hide away by myself among the trees, stand there like a dwarf with a broken heart among the giants of the forest. How can I describe to you the taste of the light wind as it makes the leaves ripple like the flags of happy nations? Just as they would sit in the sauna to make their bodies sweat and reinvigorate themselves, I would sit there alone for hours so that the salt of my body would find its way out and dissolve, so that I could say to the creatures of the forest: 'I am your sister in this existence', so that I might plant my kisses upon it. I leaped around the trees shouting and addressing the green silence around me, but I felt that my words were vanishing like smoke, and neither the trees nor even the birds were listening to me. There was a husky sadness in my voice, a scratch in the innocence of what I wanted to express, because my voice was not in tune with the sounds of the forest. Perhaps my years of hanging around in the city had tainted the purity of my powers of expression. My voice was reminiscent of the city's own symphony of mediocrity, the soulless, broken music produced by the machine of life: those sounds they have spattered us with shamelessly since childhood; their symphony that starts squeaking in the early morning, in shopping centres, banks, universities, hospitals, parliament buildings, bars and restaurants. The sounds of human ignominy. They're incapable of loving each other so how can they understand our love for them? I felt that my mind was packed with sounds – the voices on buses and trains, the noises in planes and ships, the sound of domestic disputes, insults, abuse, the whistle of bullets, shouting, screaming, weeping, the chants of environmental protesters. Applause at the Peace Prize award ceremony at a time when new wars are breaking out in new hotspots, the sound of cars crashing, car bombs exploding, the cars of thieves, an ambulance, a bank truck loaded with bundles of banknotes, a fire engine. The sounds of mosques and churches, of Friday sermons and homilies, of group sex and glass breaking, sounds coming in the right ear and sounds going out the left ear. If we were deaf creatures – us and those humans – perhaps the world would be less painful. There are only two kinds of sound that are good for bringing about peace: the songs of the forest and music. Yes, Beto, the forest is a sound. An ancient sound that renews itself like a river that never stops flowing. They have polluted the river. They have cut down the trees. They have flown into space looking for more sounds and sources of energy. They have destroyed their own humanity. They have cooked and baked and killed like mass murderers. They have given prizes and bravery awards to madmen and killers. They really are heroes. Don't they deserve hanging at the end of the film, like heroes? The audience will cry because they can't save the hero who's being hanged in the middle of the square. They have cut their humanity's throat from ear to ear and sat down weeping at its feet. They have created poems for the dignity of humanity, while others created long wars that have yet to end, and perhaps never will. Their poems are awash with shame and loss, and they still smile like clowns. Pessimistic as usual, you'll say, 'I know that'. I want to borrow your tone of wisdom, which is comical much of the time, and say, 'Humanity is in two parts, humanity has two voices. The majority talk incessantly and the minority are silent and plant-like, communicating with gestures. Every painting, Beto, is a voice. Every novel, every story, every work of art is a voice that communicates by gestures.' They are creative innovators, but they are corrupt to the core. You know, in the forest, thoughts of suicide recurred. I imagined the sharp blade of a knife against my throat. Only the forest stood between me and what I was thinking. Nonsense, nonsense, nonsense. I imagine you nosing up to me as usual and whispering, 'There you are, jumping from one subject to another like a kangaroo.'

You're quite right. I love you and miss you, Beto.

The next day they chose to go to the lake and fish, under the supervision of Miko Lahm of course, because he was the expert and we could learn from him. But Marko, my owner, didn't like his friends' plan and decided to stay at home. He spoke sharply to Paulina, then went to his room. I don't know why he hates her. Perhaps he wanted to sleep with her. I decided to stay with him in the house. We probably felt like customers at a cafe – we would sit together but each of us would live in his own labyrinthine world, with his own concerns. When they left, nobody paid any attention to Marko. I wanted to share my sense that something was troubling him and tell them all why he was depressed. But I swallowed the idea, because being obtrusive makes some of them more depressed. The Finns don't speak much or ask many questions. I tell you, this country, with the cold, the snow and the silence, suits me more than anywhere else. It's as if the environment and the introverted people here were made to measure for my temperament. I so much wanted to tell Marko that Finland was a big icy shirt that fit me well. All I needed was a glimmer of light. A slight human touch would have been enough to dress my wounds. But Marko didn't need me or anything other than himself. He humiliated me from the moment I arrived here till the end. In his company I suffered from very strange nightmares. I had no choice. I imagined life on the mean streets again, and the loss of face, in your eyes and the eyes of others, if I decided to go back.

I lived with him for a year and a half like a pampered slave. From the start he paid lots of money to put me up. He got me a passport and spent lavishly on my food and other needs, but he was damned miserly when it came to interacting with me. He wasn't interested in me. I was like any of the hundreds of old things that packed the dirty studio where we lived. I already told you he was an artist. His beard almost reached his waist. He had shaved his head and wore red trousers and shabby sports shoes. He had two shirts – one black and one blue. The only valuable thing he owned was an Italian bicycle, which was old but rare. He was crazy about buying things from secondhand shops. His studio was like a rubbish dump. We could hardly move inside it. I didn't even understand his bohemianism – it struck me as contradictory. At first I felt he had brought me to his town in order to relieve his bitter loneliness, but my presence alongside him was just a message, or a wall he set up between himself and others. He would take me along to bars, out in the streets and to the shops, just to prove that he was different from others or perhaps to challenge their fears of anything strange or different. We would often sit in the park for hours, and all he would do was watch people as they looked at us, or answer with a few brief words when one of them came up and asked what country I came from. I was like a totemic mask a tourist brought out for small children. We didn't play or have fun in those beautiful gardens. The conversation between us was sparse. Sometimes he would say a few words about how dark the winter is in Finland and sometimes he would remind me of the difference between the heat of the sun in Finland and the heat of the sun in my city. His silence, or the way he spoke so rarely, it reminded me of myself when I was very young. At that age I wouldn't speak for days on end. I had had trouble pronouncing some sounds, and when I opened my mouth, I sounded like a foreigner learning Spanish.

Marko was just a scratch on one of his mysterious paintings. That's how I started to imagine him: a scratch on a canvas painted white. Perhaps a grey scratch, like the trace of a cat's claw or the fingernail of a man smothered with a pillow. Believe me, Beto, as long as there's imagination, there's crime.

When I started imagining Marko as a scratch on a painting, I wanted to get inside his mind. One's imagination, if constantly enriched, can reach many secret places, including the imaginations and minds of others. Isn't that what we were taught in the Wise Tails school? I spent more than half an hour, that day, wandering around that house in the forest. Eventually I sloped up to the second floor, pushed the door open and went into his room. Marko was drinking alcohol straight from the bottle and didn't pay me any attention. I went downstairs again and had a snooze at the front door. I dreamt I was writing on the blackboard, then I started wiping white chalk all over the black surface. Then a beautiful female came in, with a tube of lipstick in her hand. She looked like the geography teacher in our first academy. She planted a kiss on my cheek and drew a thick red line on the board, then went out crying. When I opened my eyes I heard hurried footsteps on the stairs. It must be Marko. It seemed to me that this dream of mine was pure pain. He stroked my neck and staggered off to piss against the trunk of the tree. Perhaps Marko had been drawing while I was dreaming. I quickly sneaked back into his room. There was a painting on which the oil hadn't dried yet, a painting just in red. In it there was something like the eye of a wolf. It wasn't coloured differently but, instead of a brush, he had used a small knife to scrape off the red, exposing the black beneath. The scrapings were those wolf's eyes. They looked distorted, as if a shaky hand had done them.

Through the window I caught sight of Marko going into the sauna. He filled his bag with bottles of beer, took his Italian bike and a rifle from the sauna, and started whistling. I joined him and we set off into the depths of the forest. We sat down close to a giant tree and he started to clean the rifle. I was sitting close to him and thinking about the resemblance between us. We are both pessimistic and dreamy, and perhaps frightened of symbols. For sure he wouldn't pay much attention to the mind of someone like me. Perhaps he felt superior deep down, because I'm just a tramp he adopted from the streets of Ciudad del Sol. Perhaps he even sees my bohemianism as a worthless bohemianism. He's a civilized bohemian and I'm a savage bohemian. I might be wrong. Perhaps he hated my mind and perhaps he thought I was making fun of his silence and his worries. Did my being in his company expose the fragility of his life? Once he took me to a bar. It was a snowy night and a biting cold had the city in its grip. As we were going back to the studio, he slipped and fell flat on his face. I thought he had died. He was still holding my leash and I was worried I might freeze out there. I tried to revive him but he started cursing me and my past life, and making fun of the culture of Ciudad del Sol. I managed to get away from him and raced back to the bar to seek help. They carried him to the studio and I spent the night scrutinising his face. Why did he bring me into his life if it had to be walled off by all this sadness, loneliness and suspicion?

He rolled a joint and poured more beer into his belly. I examined the place around us. There were numerous trees that were quite wonderful. I was struck by a strange tree that looked like a woman on fire. I was drooling as I went around the trunk of the tree. Maybe that tree was related to the tree in the story that our friend Sancho tells. If only! I'd always wished that tree would swallow all my apprehensions, there on that mysterious island in the Pacific.

It's said to be the same island that Sindbad reached and told amazing stories about. That tree, they say, feeds on humans and other animals. The inhabitants of the island believe that the spirits of their ancestors and their gods sleep in the leaves of the tree. The tree wraps its branches around its prey and the leaves stick to their body, then suck ravenously until the prey is just a dry skeleton without a single drop of life. The inhabitants worship it and offer sacrifices to it. Every year they give it a body. The victim is chosen by means of dreams. If any of the local people dream about standing under the tree, they have to admit it to the island's priests. If anyone fails to report such a dream, a curse will pursue them for the rest of their life. So the dreamers would come forward voluntarily and give their bodies to satisfy the hunger of their ancestors and the gods.

Marko put the rifle aside. He whistled to me and I approached cautiously. He stretched out close to me and started to stroke me gently at first. His fingers were creeping between my legs. He had done it to me more than once. All my childhood came back to me as soon as his fingers touched my body. I was always on the alert and I was thinking I would bite off his penis with my teeth if he did it. But it was my cowardice that prevailed. As soon as he tried to hold me between his legs, I slipped out of his grip and ran away as fast as I could. He started shouting and threatening me, then he started firing his gun at me. He was drunk and I was terrified. I hid in the bushes, held my breath and listened to his shouts behind me. He suddenly stopped shouting and, muttering to himself, retraced his steps to where he had left his bicycle, then calm reigned around us.

I lay on my back and let out a sigh from deep inside me towards the sky. Life, life, life. Do you remember, Beto, the difference between barking and language? Their language has poisoned us. We should stick to barking, stop understanding what they say. All those metaphors and silly figures of speech. Professor Azmeh was right: mankind can put any word next to the word 'life', but when they do so the results suggest intellectual laziness. That's how they fall in love, and sing, write books and die – prisoners of their metaphors since ancient times. They repeat the same old songs: life is a journey, life is a stairway, life is a mill, a ship, a garden, a grave. Life is a book. Life is a galaxy. Life is a cage, insomnia, a cross, a disease, smoke. Life is a river, an ocean, an island. Life is a valley. Life is a mountain. Life is a hospital, a bed, a disease. Life is a womb. Life is a gramophone record. Life is a hole, a trap, life is a trench. Life is a dictionary. Life is a gospel. Life is a poem. Life is a comedy, a painting, music. Life is a dream. Life is an itch. Life is a swing. Life is a gallows. There's no word that can't be coupled with the word 'life'. Life is shit. Life is a prison. Life is cinema. There's no word, whatever form it may take and whatever it may mean, that can't go with the word 'life' without meaning something, without leading to the essence of life. Because life is garbage and a flower at the same time. If there was one word that didn't go with 'life', that word would be the key to the secret of these humans. Just one word. O Lord of Shit, there isn't one word that can't be added mathematically without leading to a similar result: life is a street, life is poison, life is a cloud, life is a tunnel, life is a toilet...

I jumped out of the bushes as if driven by some wild animal energy. I tracked his scent. I kept barking all the way, running like mad. I reached the edge of the lake. His friends had left the place. He was floating in the lake, drunk and singing. I kept barking at him for more than five minutes. He started waving his hand at me. I wanted to grab him by the neck. I jumped into the water and started swimming around him. He was shouting out ecstatically and his voice echoed from every direction. I dived down under him, grabbed the end of his trouser leg and pulled him down until he stopped breathing.

These humans, Beto.

We who bark.

You and I, and this world, I wish everything would disappear, except my memories. I want the memories to remain dead in some place and forever, like the smell of piss on the trunk of a tree.

Please, Beto.

Forgive me.

The Killers and the Compass

ABU HADID KNOCKED back what remained of the bottle of arak. He put his face close to mine and, with the calm of someone high on hashish, gave me this advice: 'Listen, Mahdi. I've seen all kinds of problems in my life and I know that one day I'll run out of luck. You're sixteen, and today I'm going to teach you how to be a lion. In this world you need to be street-smart. Whether you die today or in thirty years, it doesn't make any difference. It's today that matters and whether you can see the fear in people's eyes. People who are frightened will give you everything. If someone tells you "God forbids it" or "That's wrong", for example, give him a kick up the arse, because that god's full of shit. That's their god, not your god. *You* are your own god and this is your day. There's no god without followers or cry-babies willing to die of hunger or suffer in his name. You have to learn how to make yourself God in this world, so that people lick your arse while you shit down their throats. Don't open your mouth today, not a word. You come with me, dumb as a lamb. Understand, dickhead?'

He thumped the arak bottle against the wall and aimed a friendly punch hard into my nose.

We walked through the darkness of the muddy lanes. The wretched houses were catching their breath after receiving a whipping from the storm. Inside them the people were sleeping and dreaming. Everything was soaked and knocked out of place. The wind that had toyed with the labyrinth of lanes all evening, picked up strength, then finally left with a bitter chill hanging over the place – this sodden neighbourhood where I would live and die. Many times I imagined the neighbourhood as if it were some offspring of my mother's. It smelled that way and was just as miserable. I don't recall ever seeing my mother as a human being. She would always be weeping and wailing in the corner of the kitchen like a dog tied up to be tormented. My father would assail her with a hail of insults and when her endurance broke, she would whine aloud: 'Why, good Lord? Why? Take me and save me.'

Only then would my father stand up, take the cord out of his headdress and whip her non-stop for half an hour, spitting at her throughout.

My nose was bleeding profusely. I was holding my head back as I tried to keep pace with Abu Hadid. The smell of spiced fish wafted from the window of Majid the traffic policeman's house. He must have been blind drunk to be frying fish in the middle of the night. We turned down a narrow, winding lane. Abu Hadid picked up a stone and threw it towards two cats that were fighting on top of a pile of rubbish. They jumped through the window of Abu Rihab's abandoned house. The rubbish almost reached the roof of the place. The government had executed Abu Rihab and confiscated his house. They say his family went back to the country where their clan lived. Abu Rihab had been in contact with the banned Daawa Party. After a year of torture and interrogation in the vaults of the security services, he was branded a traitor and shot. It was impossible to forget the physical presence of his beautiful daughter, Rihab. She was a carbon copy of Jennifer Lopez in *U Turn*. I'd seen the film at the home of Abbas, the poet who lived next door. He had films that wouldn't be shown on state television for a hundred years. Most of the young men in the neighbourhood had tried to court Rihab with love letters, but she was an idiot who understood nothing but washing the courtyard and pouring water over the hands of her Daawa Party father before he prayed.

Abu Hadid, my giant brother, stopped in front of the door to Umm Hanan's house. She was the widow of Allawi

Shukr and people in the neighbourhood made fun of her morals by calling her Hanan Aleena, which means something like 'easy favours'. We went inside and sat on a wooden bench with an uncomfortable back. Umm Hanan asked one of her daughters to wash my face and take care of me. The girl blocked my nose with cotton wool. Umm Hanan had three beautiful daughters, all alike as nurses in uniform. My brother slept with Umm Hanan. Then he fucked her youngest daughter twice. After that he told Umm Hanan to fuck me. I was surprised he didn't ask that of the girl who was my age. Then Abu Hadid took some money and three packets of cigarettes from Umm Hanan, and gave me one of the packets. We set off again, walking along the muddy lanes. Abu Hadid slowed down, then retraced his steps and stopped at the door of Abu Mohammed, the car mechanic. He knocked on the door with his foot. The man came out in his white dishdasha with his paunch sticking out. His eyes popped out of his head when Abu Hadid greeted him. Me and the other kids used to call him 'the gerbil who swallowed the watermelon'. He used to give me and the gang pills in return for puncturing the tyres of cars in the neighbourhood, so that his business would flourish. We would bargain with him over how many pills for how many tyres. My brother ordered me to take off my bloodied shirt and told the mechanic to fetch me a clean one. The gerbil obeyed at once and came back with a blue shirt that smelled of soap. It was the shirt his son, a student at medical college, had just been wearing. I was surprised that the size fit me exactly. My brother leaned over and whispered a few words in the mechanic's ear, and the mechanic's face turned even darker than usual.

We crossed the main street towards the other neighbourhood. All along the way I was wondering what Abu Hadid had whispered in the gerbil's ear. Abu Hadid coughed loudly and his chest wheezed like my uncle's old tractor. He didn't say a single word on the way. He lit two cigarettes at the same time and offered one to me. It was after midnight. I don't know anyone who lives in this neighbourhood, other than an obnoxious boy who was at school with us. He once punched me and I never did manage to stick a finger up his arse in return. When he found out I was Abu Hadid's brother, his father came to school and asked me to beat his son up. People were scared senseless of my brother's brutality. His reputation for ruthless delinquency spread throughout the city. He would baffle the police and other security agencies for many years until, that is, the day he was executed in public. Even his enemies mourned him when the inevitable happened. Occasionally in life he had defended people, against the cruelty of the ruling party, for example. Abu Hadid didn't distinguish between good and evil. He had his own private demons. Once he threw a hand grenade at the party office when 'the comrades' executed someone who had evaded military conscription. Another time he mutilated the face of some wretched vegetable seller, simply because he was drunk and he felt like it. Abu Hadid would go on the rampage like that for eight years, until Johnny the barber gave him away. The night it happened Abu Hadid was fucking Johnny's pretty brown daughter on the roof of the house. The police surrounded him and shot him in the leg. They executed him a week later. My mother and my seven sisters would beat their breasts for a whole year, but my father was relieved to be rid of the antics of his wayward son.

Abu Hadid knocked on a rusty door that still had a few spots of green paint, shaped like frogs, on it. We were received by a man in his forties with a thick moustache which covered his teeth when he spoke. We sat down in the guest room in front of the television. I gathered that the man lived alone. He went into the kitchen and came back with a bottle of arak. He opened it and poured a glass. My brother told him to pour one for me too. We sat in silence, and the man and I watched a football match between two local teams, while my brother stared into a small fish tank.

'Do you think the fish are happy in the tank?' my brother asked, calm and serious.

'As long as they eat and drink and swim, they're fine,' the man replied, without looking away from the television screen.

'Do fish drink water?'

'Sure they drink, of course.'

'How can fish drink saltwater?'

'Sure they have a way. How could they be in water and not drink?'

'If they're in water, perhaps they don't need to drink.'

'Why don't you ask the fish in the tank?'

Before the bald man could turn to look at him, my brother had jumped on top of him like a hungry tiger. He threw him to the ground, squatted on his chest and pinned his arms down under his knees. In a flash he took a small knife out of his pocket, put it close to the man's eye and started shouting hysterically in his face: 'Answer, you cocksucker! How can fish drink saltwater? Answer, you son of a bitch! Answer! Do fish drink water or don't they? Answer, shit-for-brains!'

Abu Hadid stuck a cucumber up the man's arse and we left the house. I never would understand what the man had to do with my brother. We headed towards the car park. A thin young man, a year younger than my brother, was leaning against a red Chevrolet Malibu dating from the seventies. He embraced my brother warmly and I felt that Abu Hadid and he were genuine friends. We set off in the car, smoking and listening to a popular song about lovers parting. We took the highway towards the outskirts of the city. Abu Hadid turned off the tape player, lay back in his seat and said, 'Murad, tell my brother the story about the Pakistani kid.'

'Sure, no problem,' replied Murad Harba.

'Listen, Mahdi. Some years back I took the plunge and escaped to Iran. I was thinking of going from there into Turkey and putting this fucked-up country behind me. I lived in a filthy house in the north of Iran, with people coming from Pakistan, Afghanistan and Iraq and everywhere on God's pimping Earth. We waited for them to hand us over to the Iranian trafficker who was going to take us across the mountainous border. That's where I met the Pakistani kid. He was about your age, nice guy, young and very handsome. He spoke little Arabic but he had memorised the Quran. He was always scared. And he had a strange object in his possession: a compass. He would hold it in the palm of his hand like a butterfly and stare at it. Then he would hide it in a special pouch that hung around his neck like a golden pendant. He hanged himself in the bathroom the day before Iranian security raided the house. They shoved us in jail and beat us up plenty. When they'd finished humiliating us, we got our breath back and started to get to know the other prisoners. One of the people we chatted with was a young Iraqi who'd been jailed for selling hashish. He was born in Iran. The government had deported his family from Baghdad after the war broke out on the grounds that he had Iranian nationality. I told him about the Pakistani kid who had hanged himself. The man was really upset about the poor boy, said he had met him before, that he was a good kid, and that he knew the whole story of the compass.

'In 1989 in the Pakistani city of Peshawar, Sheikh Abdullah Azzam, the spiritual father of the jihad in Afghanistan, was in a car on his way to pray in a mosque frequented by the Afghan Arabs – the Arabs who went to fight in Afghanistan. The car was blown up as it crossed a bridge over a storm drain. His two sons were with him and were torn to pieces. According to the muezzin[5] of the mosque, who rushed to the scene of the explosion as soon as it happened, Azzam's body was seemingly untouched. Not a single scratch. There was just a thin line of blood running from the corner of the dead sheikh's mouth. It was a dreadful disaster – al Qaeda was accused of assassinating the sheikh who had stood up to the might of the Soviet Union, perhaps to give them greater impunity as an organisation.

5. Muezzin - the person who calls muslims to prayer from the minaret.

'Before many others had gathered, Malik the muezzin spotted the compass close to the wreckage of the car. When he wiped the blood off it, he felt a shiver run up his spine. It was an army compass with the words Allah and Muhammad engraved on it. It was clear to the muezzin that it was the sheikh's holy compass, blessed by God and a conduit for His miracles. Many of the mujahideen claimed the compass turned blood-red when God intended good or evil for the person carrying it. Azzam had never parted with it throughout his life in jihad. Malik hid it at home for ten years. He took it out every night, polished it and looked at it, as he shed tears of sorrow at the death of the mujahideen's sheikh.

'The muezzin placed the compass gently into the hand of his son Waheed, like someone setting down a precious jewel onto a piece of cloth. Waheed had decided to smuggle his way into England. He might strike lucky there, help his family and study to become a doctor. The muezzin told his son Waheed the secret of the compass and advised him to guard it with his life. With firm faith, he told him the compass would help him on his journey and throughout his life, and that it was the most precious thing a father could offer his son. Waheed was unaware of the compass's powers and significance, and didn't know much about those holy and special moments when the compass turned red to warn of good or evil, but his faith in his father made him treasure it. The compass then became inseparable from his person. Waheed reached Iran and lived in dilapidated houses run by traffickers. He had to work six months to save enough money to make the crossing to Turkey. One day he went out with six young Afghans to work on a building site. A rich Iranian man picked them up in a small truck and drove them to the outskirts of the town, where he was building an enormous house in the middle of his farm. They were working for a pittance. The man dropped them off at his farm and asked them to clear away the bricks, plaster, sacks and wood left over from the building work. The deal was that the owner would come back late that evening and take them back to town. He gave them half their wages in advance and advised them to finish the work properly. Waheed and the Afghans worked slowly and lazily all day long. When the sun set they all prayed and then sat down to relax in one of the large rooms. They poured some juice, rolled cigarettes and started to chat about trafficking routes to Europe. Every now and then the young Afghans would give Waheed sly looks of contempt. The owner was late. The Afghans decided to pass the time by playing a betting game, which was really a malicious trick. There was a group of barrels filled with water, next to some bags full of plaster. They told Waheed the game was that they would mix the plaster with water in a barrel and everyone in the group would put his hands in the mixture up to his elbow, and whoever managed to keep them in the longest would win a sum of money. They suggested Waheed go first. Full of good cheer and innocence, Waheed stood up and went through the motions, burying his arms in the plaster mixture. Within a few minutes the plaster set hard and Waheed's arms were trapped in the barrel. The Afghans pulled down Waheed's trousers and raped him one by one.'

Between us we smoked nine cigarettes while listening to the story about the Pakistani. Murad Harba spat out his tale in one burst, then drank from the bottle of water next to him, cursing God. Abu Hadid took his pistol out of his belt and started to load it with bullets. The story about the Pakistani had no effect on me. I was entranced by the company of my brother Abu Hadid and by the chance to enter his various worlds. We turned off into an extensive park with bare trees like soldiers turned to stone. Murad switched off the engine. My heart was starting to pound and I was curious to find out what they would do in the darkness of the cold park. Obviously we hadn't come all this way to listen to the story about the Pakistani. We got out of the car. Abu Hadid looked around while Murad Harba opened the boot of the car and took out a pick and shovel. Abu Hadid ordered me to help Murad dig. My blood began to race with excitement and fear. Abu Hadid, with his strong muscles, helped with the digging. We began to sweat. The ground was tough. The tangled roots of a tree and a large stone hampered our work. Before we'd had time to catch our breath, Murad and Abu Hadid headed back to the boot of the car, while I stood close to the hole, bewildered like a deaf man at a wedding party. They took a man, bound and gagged, out of the boot and dragged him along the ground to the hole. My brother told me to come close and look into the man's eyes. The look of fear I saw is stamped in my memory as though with a branding iron. Abu Hadid kicked him in the back and the man slumped into the hole. We shovelled soil on top of him and levelled the ground well.

Abu Hadid gave my hair a sharp tug and whispered in my ear:

'Now you're God.'

Why Don't You Write a Novel, Instead of Talking About All These Characters?

WE BROUGHT A half-naked Afghan corpse with us. Adel Salim and I dragged it for three cruel nights through a forest that appeared to be endless, with no way out. Adel had taken off the Afghan's black shirt and I'd tied his feet together with the sleeves. It was the last forest before the Romanian-Hungarian border. After ten yards the shirt had torn and from then on we had to drag him by the arms. It had been snowing since we crossed the river, but lying there on that final night, I forgot all this and dreamt I was sleeping in the cells of my military unit from the war days. At dawn we woke to the sight of Hungarian army dogs sniffing the Afghan's corpse.

Your name?

Salem Hussein.

Age?

Thirty.

The woman made a hand gesture, telling me to take off my underpants. Yesterday they took our stool samples, today they're examining our skin. She made a note in the papers in front of her, then made a little upward gesture with her finger. I pulled up my underpants. She waved towards the door without looking up at me. I put on the rest of my clothes. Adel Salim came in after me, then a tall young Nigerian called James. He was wearing summer shorts with a smiley face printed on the backside and a thin shirt in the colours of the Jamaican flag. He protested to the escort when she told him he couldn't go outside for a smoke. The only ones left were the Moroccan, and an old Kurdish man and his wife. We were a new group of inmates. We had reached the hospital early in the morning escorted by a pretty young woman called Anisa from the refugee reception centre. She was an Albanian who had got a job at the centre after living there as a refugee for five years and, in the meantime, had become fluent in Hungarian. We were each given a container for a stool sample and a plastic tube for urine. The Moroccan stood up and undid his trouser belt a little, tucked in his red sports shirt and then fastened the belt tight. James the Nigerian came out of the doctor's room ecstatic, and pulled the cord of his shorts, as if he had just come out of a prostitute's room. Anisa said the nurse would come soon to collect the urine and stool samples and she hoped the tests would go well. Out of the blue she told us what had happened to the previous group. That was a month earlier. She said they were ten young Somali men with a young boy. One of them took all the stool containers and filled them himself, while the others only filled the urine bottles. Of course in the laboratory they could easily tell that all the stool samples came from one man. When they were challenged on this, the Somalis pleaded that they couldn't find any other way to fill the containers. They said they struggled to procure a sample from the Western-style toilets because the shit bobbed about in the water and it was hard to fish it out. So one of them took on the task. He shat on the bathroom floor and with that filled all the containers easily, including the boy's.

Adel Salim and I had arrived three days after the others. They gave us a quick interrogation at the army post on the border and in the morning they sent us to a refugee reception centre in a border town. I don't know where they took the corpse of the Afghan. They told us that after the medical tests the police and the immigration department would question us again on the details of how he died. They put us in the quarantine section of the reception centre, a small building attached to the main centre where the rest of the inmates were staying. The Hungarians call it the 'karanten', similar to the Iraqi version of the word – 'karantina'. It was dirty and crowded with Afghans, Arabs, Kurds, Pakistanis, Sudanese, Bangladeshis, Africans and some Albanians. The tests went on for a month. The frightening aspect of the quarantine section was the results of the medical tests, because some of the refugees had tuberculosis or scabies. Those ones were transferred from the quarantine section to the isolation hospital on the outskirts of the town. They would stay there until they were cured. That is what most of the new inmates feared most: not the disease but the time they would need to stay for treatment, which could be more than a year and a half. The Iraqis and Iranians made fun of tuberculosis and scabies because they thought they only infected Bangladeshis, Pakistanis, Afghans and Africans. In fact the test results seemed to confirm this, and the diseases of the Iraqis, the Iranians and the Kurds proved to be exclusively venereal, in particular gonorrhoea, which could be treated within the reception centre.

We had crossed the Romanian-Hungarian border with a professional trafficker. At dawn he'd told us that the fog had started to thicken and we would have to stick together to reach the river and then cross the river into Hungarian territory. The trafficker said he had no obligation to wait for anyone who stopped walking and we would keep going until the fog lifted. We did our best to keep up with the trafficker. We swore to the interrogators that the Afghan died crossing the river. He had been very ill, and he soon drowned and we couldn't save him, but the medical reports showed he had died of strangulation. I told them honestly and faithfully what had happened that foggy morning. The trafficker had lost his way (that's what he told us), so he said we had to spend the night in the forest. We got into our sleeping bags, shivering from the cold – you can ask James the Nigerian, the Moroccan or the old Kurd, because they crossed before us and they explained what happened next when we met them in the quarantine centre. It was a shabby trick. The trafficker knew that the river was one kilometre from the forest, but the boat that one of his assistants from the Romanian border villages had left for us would only hold five people, so the trafficker would have to abandon three of us. I'm sure he was aware of the boat problem in advance, before the journey even began in Bucharest. The trafficker waited till about half an hour after we had got into our sleeping bags, then started going round the group, kicking each one gently, in the expectation that only some would wake up. This selection method of his succeeded. Adel Salim, the Afghan and I were fast asleep, while the others were dozing or couldn't sleep at all for the cold. So they left us in the forest, dead to the world. When we woke up we realised we'd been tricked. We started looking for the river so we could cross into Hungary ourselves. God started making the fog even thicker. He seemed to be doing it deliberately. Hours later we reached the river. The cold had exhausted the Afghan and he no longer had the strength to walk. He had a raging fever. Adel very much liked the Afghan, and the two of us carried him. The poor man had stuck with us and become a companion and a brother since we met him crossing the mountains on the Iranian-Turkish border. Adel asked me to cross the river first, to try out the crossing, and then call them from the other bank to explain to them how to cross without getting lost in the fog. Adel said he would help the Afghan by himself. Shivering from the intense cold, I shouted out to Adel from the far bank. Then I heard him jump into the water with the Afghan. I shouted out to show them the way and after a while I heard them splashing around in the water. Adel shouted that the Afghan had started to drown. I shouted out again, begging him not to abandon him. The sound of them splashing in the water quickly grew louder, then suddenly everything was quiet. I was about to jump back into the water to help them when I saw Adel emerging from the fog, pulling the Afghan after him, dead. Adel burst out crying and I decided not to leave the Afghan's body, although Adel objected at first.

It's been three years since this incident took place. I'm now working in the refugee camp in place of Anisa the Albanian, who has returned to her own country. I work as a translator for the immigration department, and I escort the new quarantine inmates to the hospital every morning. There's nothing exciting in my life, the same shit and urine problems, the usual refusals to strip off in front of a woman doctor. I wanted to forget my countrymen, and match the rhythm of my life to the slow pace of this border town. I visit the Afghan's grave from time to time, because he was buried in the town cemetery close to the refugee reception centre. His grave is the only one without a cross. People who visit the cemetery take a look at it out of curiosity, to see the Quranic verse engraved on the headstone. I drink in the bar every evening. I sleep with a woman who works in the flower shop, who loves me very much. I read the newspaper on the internet. Sometimes I cry all night. But for the last few years I haven't dared visit the prison where Adel Salim lives in the capital, Budapest. Then one day I made up my mind to go and visit him.

The encounter only lasted a matter of minutes.

'Okay, I don't understand, Adel,' I said. 'What were you thinking? Why did you strangle him? What I'm saying may be mad, but why didn't you let him drown by himself?'

After a short while, he answered hatefully from behind the bars. 'You're an arsehole and a fraud. Your name's Hassan Blasim and you claim to be Salem Hussein. You come here and lecture me. Go fuck yourself, you prick.'

He blew out a lungful of cigarette smoke and went back to his cell.

On the train back I was bewildered and there was a bitter taste in my mouth. I wanted to sleep but my mind was seething. I tried to put the events of my life in order, but many of them had faded into oblivion: my first meeting with Adel Salim in the south of the country, our plan to escape from the military lock-up, the Iranian border guards who arrested us, the electric-shock torture, meeting the Afghan, the river, Hassan Blasim, the border. The train stopped at a station. I went to the bathroom and when I came back a fat man had taken a seat in the compartment. Next to him he had a small cage with a white mouse inside. He looked up from his newspaper. I greeted him. He nodded and went back to his newspaper.

The train set off and the man put out his hand.

'My name's Saro,' he said. 'My wife gave me this beautiful mouse. It's my birthday. Fifty years old.'

'Salem Hussein,' I said and shook his hand.

'That's strange,' said the man, examining my face. 'I've read many of your stories. You're a writer!'

'That must be someone else,' I said. 'I don't have anything to do with writing. I'm a translator in the immigration department. It's true I wrote some poems in my youth, but I've never written anything else.'

'Perhaps... perhaps you'll write something later,' he said.

He folded his newspaper and added, 'I was born in the Year of the Mouse.' He started telling me about the Chinese Zodiac, and said that people born in the Year of the Mouse like to talk about themselves and the way they live. They are very kind but they are also very ambitious, and it's hard for them to get on with people born in other years. They love debate and their biggest problem is their selfishness. I gathered he had chosen the Year of the Mouse for himself because he was so interested in mice, and not because of his real date of birth. He described the mouse as a gentle and fascinating creature, and we started chatting about mice and their qualities, as the man had extensive experience in all things mouse-related. The conversation led me to expound on my own life and on what had happened with Adel Salim and the Afghan. I started to humour his passion for mice and I told him what I could remember: in my childhood we lived in an area called Air Force Square, close to a military airfield. It was a dirty area teeming with mice, cockroaches and flies. Everyone tried to get rid of the mice, but in vain. My elder sister, like the rest of the women, would set small wooden traps in the kitchen. When a mouse went into the trap it would end up scalded. My sister would boil some water and pour it on top of the mouse – a special form of extermination. It was a horrible death. The smell of boiled mouse hung in the courtyard for more than a day. My grandfather had his own method. He had a long stick at the end of which he had hammered in some nails, and with a quick flick he would hit the mouse, which would start bleeding and make a horrible squealing noise. My sister never accepted this method, because the floor would get spattered with blood and, like the other women in the neighbourhood, she preferred boiled mice to bleeding mice.

'Permit me to tell you that you're lying. These are not memories. Doesn't what you say come from a story called 'My Wife's Bottom'?'

'If you say so, Mr Saro,' I said, shifting in my seat.

The man looked at me calmly and said, 'Listen, young man. Can you tell me, for example, who wrote 'The Killers and the Compass'? It's the one about the Pakistani kid who finds a sacred compass, and tells how he carried it from Pakistan to Iran, and the rape incident. Your friend Adel Salim killed the Afghan to obtain the compass. It sounds like a riddle or a silly detective story. I'm sure you'll clear the matter up in another story. Why don't you write a novel, instead of talking about all these characters – Arabs, Kurds, Pakistanis, Sudanese, Bangladeshis and Africans? They would make for mysterious, traditional stories. Why do you cram all these names into one short story? Let the truth come to light in all its simplicity. Why not enjoy your life?'

'Mr Saro, I don't understand what you're saying. Besides, you're talking about truth and for a start I hate anyone who utters that word as if he's a prophet or a god. Maybe you've heard of Jalal ad-Din Rumi, the Sufi Muslim who died in 1273. Rumi says, "The truth was once a mirror in the hands of God. Then it fell and broke into a thousand pieces. Everybody has a very small piece of it, but each one believes he has the whole truth."'

Saro said, 'I know your friend Rumi but I've never heard of him saying that. Listen, mice are colour blind, but they can distinguish shading, from black through to white, and that's enough to get a grip on some reality.'

Then Saro stopped talking and left me to myself. He took a lump of cheese out of his bag and started to break it up into small pieces, which he threw at the mouse in the cage.

'Mr Saro, you seem to be a foreigner like me.' I said.

'It's true. I'm from Turkey,' he said, looking at his mouse.

'It's a beautiful country.'

'Really?' said Saro.

'Definitely.'

'You cursed your time there. You ate shit in Istanbul, as you put it. You worked like a donkey in restaurants and factories for a pittance,' said Saro.

I examined his face in the hope of uncovering his personality.

'We didn't meet in the way you imagine. Everything exists in stories,' said Saro.

'We're going back to the subject of writing again.'

'Why not? It's an impressive human activity,' said Saro.

'Let me ask you, Mr Saro. Are you interested in literature? Do you write?'

'No, I'm only interested in the lives of mice.'

The train stopped again. Mr Saro put on his coat, picked up his mouse and left.

Then he came back and stuck his head through the compartment door. 'Why didn't you mention your real name in this story?' he asked. 'Your friend Rumi said, "There is no imagination in the world without truth."'

'Rumi also says, "You saw the image but you missed the meaning,"' I answered. I wanted to ask him not to leave me on my own.

'But I hate rats,' came Saro's reply.

The train moved. My tooth was hurting. I took an aspirin and tried to relax. I browsed through the newspaper without interest. On the back page there was a story about a poisoning incident:

A Belgian woman set sail on a boating expedition last week, accompanied by only her dog and a few cans of her favourite drink, Coca Cola. Once out in clear water, the woman stowed her cans in the boat's refrigerator and then, according to police reports, began to play with the dog by vigorously rubbing its penis. The next day the woman was taken to hospital and put in intensive care. She died three days later. After a post-mortem examination, and prior to the dog being handed over to a shelter for stray pets, it was established that rat urine on the Coca Cola cans was the cause of the illness, having infected the woman with a deadly spirochaetic-related pathogen. As part of the investigation police and public health officials have now visited the supermarket where the woman purchased the cans. The rat is still being sought.

Sarsara's Tree

SITTING ON TOP of the hill under a tree... Typing my remarks about the River Nabi on a laptop... A giant sun roasts the village. Ants carry away the remains of a dead hornet. Other strange insects nibble at each other. My stomach hurts! The doctor says it's an inflammation of the colon. My stomach swelled up three weeks ago as if I were pregnant. I'm writing a study for a local NGO that intends to rip off a foreign NGO that issues grants. My task is to exaggerate the truth. To spread panic about drought. To paint a bleak picture of the many villages that lie scattered along the banks of the River Nabi, which runs between my country and that of our hostile neighbours. We've been fighting ruinous wars with these neighbours since the dawn of history. The fragile peace we now have with them is just a dormant volcano. I'm currently contributing to a narrative that concludes with the volcano erupting once again. Without water blood will flow. Thirst will arouse that brutal, hostile memory. And it won't be just humans that will perish, but also rare birds and insects and the flocks of animals that provide the local people with their sustenance, not to mention the rhythm of their lives.

This year I've toured six villages and recorded my dramatic observations on each one. Sarsara's village, which faces the River Nabi, was my last fact-finding destination. This is the great river of whose banks poets have sung countless praises. Each, in his own language, offered to its sweet waters love, reverence, rituals, fabulous stories and reports of floods and drownings. What does our NGO want to prove? If the river runs dry it will be filled with the blood of those who love it. Water is love. The spectre of the future takes the form of a terrifying desert. We won't go back to the jungle to fight. This time we'll go to the desert and slaughter each other. Our new ice age will be a thirsty desert.

The birds don't land on Sarsara's tree and the insects don't climb it. That's what the teacher said and that's what I noticed during the three hours I spent close by. I took some pictures of the tree and kept a twig from one of the branches.

I met the village teacher after fruitless meetings with some of the local people. They would talk like cartoon characters. They were pleasant and generous, but their vagueness was annoying. I had doubts about everything Mr Shamreen, the village teacher, told me. He may have been in collusion with our NGO. For all I knew, he may have received a bribe to make up stories about the drought. What he told me about Sarsara's tree didn't answer my questions about the harvests and the water problems. Sure, he was a friendly, educated man. But he struck me as somewhat devious. The local people consulted him on everything, large or small. When I visited him in his mud room, where he taught reading and writing, he had an adolescent boy with him. The boy had big eyes that sparkled brightly at me. The boy was consulting him about the purple flowers that surrounded the village like an arc every spring. He was asking why the bees avoided these flowers. Shamreen replied that the bees were upset because a distinctive star had disappeared from the firmament recently. And the bees would come back soon when they were sure that the star was safely on its path to a new life. The boy suggested they all support the bees in their sadness and in their work to look after the star by agreeing with the birds that the farmers and the birds would refrain from singing throughout the coming spring.

The local people spoke in this way about most aspects of their life. From what I gathered, they avoided bad luck by using a special language. They had invented this language after the Sarsara incident. Shamreen the teacher was the only one authorized to speak to outsiders in the common tongue. And this Shamreen decided to speak to me on condition that I didn't interrupt him with lots of questions. In fact I wasn't interested in their secrets or their fables. Most of the villages were teeming with fables and strange stories. And then, if Shamreen was honest in what he said, why would he reveal their secrets to me? All I hoped to do was finish writing the report and submit my resignation from this thieving NGO. Their main concern, after all, was to convince international institutional donors that global warming would have a decisive effect on the drought problem and that the complicated political relationship with our neighbours could lead to problems in the near future, especially as our country's rivers have their sources in neighbouring states. As far as I was concerned, the picture was clear: corruption and mismanagement of water resources. Large amounts of water were wasted because of the outdated methods the farmers used when irrigating their fields. But our organisation would gain nothing from this analysis. It was only panic about drought that would bring the money in. Talking up nightmare scenarios is a commercial venture that generally succeeds.

Shamreen the teacher had been an adolescent when the old woman Sarsara went off on her last grazing expedition. She had already lost her only son when he was twenty. He had taken his boat and rowed far out into the river to catch fish. He wasn't a skilled fisherman. Many of the village people go fishing from time to time, but most of them are wheat farmers and a few live by herding animals. Sarsara's son, a herdsman, drowned in the river in mysterious circumstances. The people who lived in Shams village brought his bloated body back from the other bank of the river.

'Is it possible that the people on the other bank killed him?' I asked the teacher.

'No, the people in Shams don't interfere in human affairs,' he said.

'Don't interfere in human affairs!'

'Well, I don't mean they're not human. But they don't interfere in matters of life and death...That's another subject... I'm talking to you about the tree... I'll get to that story,' said the teacher.

Sarsara mourned for her son quietly, as if a sparrow had died at the sunset hour. We buried her only son in the village cemetery and went back to our daily concerns. Sarsara looked after her son's sheep and started to live in seclusion, protected by an aura of respect. One day Sarsara went out to graze her animals in the direction of the southern pastures on the way to the desert. She loaded her tent and some provisions on her donkey and set off with twenty sheep and three dogs. This trip to the pastures would normally last three days. But Sarsara didn't come back to the village for five years. A military intelligence unit found her in the middle of the desert, all alone in her tent with only a cockerel for company. When they asked her what she was doing in such a desolate spot, she couldn't give a straight answer. All she said was that her son had died and she had this cockerel. Then she said that she sometimes received supplies of water and food from the bedouin nomads in the desert. The intelligence officer said he would take her to hospital to check her health first. Sarsara came straight back to him with a request.

'I want to swim in the River Nabi,' she said.

The intelligence unit took her to the city. They took care of her and checked all the villages on the banks of the River Nabi until they identified her village, which at the time was named after the river – Nabi village.

The villagers were delighted to see her back. Tears flowed and they embraced her like a spoiled child. But the old woman didn't recognise them. She treated them as if they were apparitions. For her the river was the only truth. She pointed towards it, then ran like a cheerful little girl and jumped into it. She swam and sang old songs the ancestors had sung hundreds of years ago. The villagers accepted Sarsara's new status gladly and with love. They left her to strip off, swim in the river, joke and play, and they took care of her food and clothing. But they couldn't persuade her to live in either her old house or any other house. As soon as she tired of the river she would stroll back towards the cattle pen and sleep there. Only a few days after Sarsara came back the trees started to appear. They were suddenly springing up everywhere from underground. They were strange trees of a kind the villages along the river had never known. Poisonous weed-like trees. The trees sprouted out of the ground, then spread and grew within minutes to a height of more than a hundred feet. They were born dead, without leaves, and their thin branches were entangled like broken cobwebs. Every tree killed the ground for half a mile around it in a circle. The soil turned to rock and no form of life survived. It was a disaster. We didn't have enough agricultural land to be able to deal with this sudden death of the soil. It wasn't long before we got to the bottom of it. The old woman Sarsara was the reason why the death trees had appeared. The local people worked together cutting down the trees. We dug up the roots and burned them. We imprisoned the old woman in the cattle pen and had a long discussion on what we should do.

We asked Sarsara to stop this strange magic of hers, because the village was threatened with ruin. But she wasn't listening. Whenever the old woman was alone and stared at the ground a tree would sprout up. She didn't understand how serious it was. She was lost in her own world. Sarsara was almost killed when the mud roof of the cattle pen fell in on her. A tree had sprouted and broken through the roof, bringing down the wooden posts. A cow and a young calf were killed.

The villagers felt sorry for Sarsara. The women baked big loaves of bread and put a flower in the middle of every loaf. The boys and girls gave out the loaves to the local people, who prayed to heaven to spare them further misfortunes through the power of the bread and the flowers.

The village elders came up with a suggestion – to blindfold Sarsara with a piece of cloth. The experiment failed. Sarsara's eyes glowed like burning coals and the piece of cloth didn't stop trees sprouting. The women wept for her and the boys and girls grew more and more anxious about the state Sarsara was in. We performed the rites and bathed in the river together after midnight. We sang all the poems we could remember about the River Nabi. The young ones decided not to embrace or kiss their fathers until their fathers took the blindfold off Sarsara's eyes.

We sent word for Hoopoe Marmour, who was wandering in the wilderness in search of himself. Marmour came from the village. He had abandoned us years earlier because of his struggle with God. He thought he was a hoopoe that had changed into a human while sleeping in a crow's nest by mistake. But a hoopoe that had not followed the path of enmity towards the villagers. He would answer any call for help. From time to time he would check to see how the villagers were because he was a wise man despite his random ravings.

Mr Marmour arrived and the villagers were relieved. Marmour went for a walk around the village side by side with Sarsara and observed her closely. As soon as the first tree sprouted, Mr Marmour said that Sarsara imagined the tree and it sprouted and it was impossible to stop this.

After what Marmour said, the villagers gathered to consult. The women and children also took part in the meeting. The debate went on till the morning. When the first rays of dawn appeared most of the people in the village had agreed to get rid of Sarsara. But the women refused to burn the old woman alive. The children suggested sending her somewhere else with the migratory birds. Marmour had asked the villagers to be patient until he could understand how her imagination worked. The discussions went on three more days until they reached a final decision.

That night we brought torches with heavy hearts. The village was sunk in sadness and fear. We took Sarsara to the hill nearest the village. We left her alone and gave her enough time to look at the ground. Sarsara's last tree sprouted, to immortalize her memory on the hill. We tied the old woman up, took her to the middle of the river in a boat and abandoned her to the waters of the Nabi.

Sunset had filled the village with a blood-red glow. The teacher advised me to stay the night because the road to the town was dangerous in the dark. He said there were armed gangs at large along the highway. I thanked Shamreen and told him I had to get home. My wife was expecting me and I had things to do early in the morning. I said goodbye to him and walked to the dirt road where I had parked the car. One thing was turning in my head: my wife naked in the shower… I would go in and press myself against her body. I was tired and I felt quite exasperated by Sarsara's village.

I tried in vain to start the car. I retraced my steps to the teacher's room to ask for help. I couldn't find him. I didn't know which house he lived in. I went to one of the nearby houses. I knocked on the door but no one answered. I pushed the door and started calling out. The house was empty. I headed to another house. The calm around me opened its mouth like a mysterious animal. Finally a young girl with dishevelled hair opened the door. 'Are you thirsty…? Tonight the foxes are going to bring lots of presents,' she said, as she took hold of my hand. I asked her where the teacher's house was and told her I needed help because my car had broken down.

She led me by the hand to the cattle pen nearby. The girl went up to a grey cow and started to milk it into a small container. Then she left the cattle pen without taking any interest in me. I followed her outside into the darkness. The village seemed to be deserted. There was just the chorus of insects gradually growing louder, as though announcing that the night and the devils were descending. The girl was heading towards the dirt road where the car was parked. I followed her, trying to feel my way in the darkness that covered Sarsara's village like an apocalypse.

The girl plucked a white flower from the side of the dirt road and threw it in the milk container.

'It's a windflower and it brings good luck,' she said, offering me the container. 'Don't eat it. Chew it, then put it in a place you've forgotten to miss.'

I drank. Then I took out the wet flower and held it

between the tips of my fingers. The girl opened the car door, pointed to the seat and then hurried off.

'Hey girl, what's your name?'

'Sarsara,' she shouted without turning back.

I checked the revolver was still in place under the seat and called my wife. As I spoke I turned the key to see if the car would start. It started immediately.

I noticed a man climbing the hill with a lantern in his hand. He hung the lantern on one of the branches of Sarsara's tree and sat down next to it. Perhaps it was the teacher. I tasted the petals of the flower with the tip of my tongue, then chewed them warily. It tasted like milk with a slightly bitter sting. I drove off at speed between the ears of corn, listening to a Sufi song about turning in the womb of the one you love.

'A place you've forgotten to miss!'

I continued on my way, thinking of places and funny incidents in my life.

The Dung Beetle

Doctor, there are stories for children and very short stories for sick people who no longer have much time. There are stories for the beach, that is to say, summer stories for women reclining in the sun topless, lazy stories about the excrement of reality, stories for the elite, for boring times, for pregnant mothers, for prisoners. I can't write a story but I can tell a story. I crave incessant talk… I have a flock of sparrows inside me… ha!

The doctor had been driving to his mother's house in a small town close to the capital. The road was slippery, because the previous day the sun had suddenly emerged from the great tent of gloom pitched above Helsinki and had melted the snow, which then turned to ice. The newspapers carried photographs of the smashed car after it had collided with the front of a school bus in which nine children were burned to death and others seriously injured. The doctor was also killed. His body had been cut in half, as if by a chainsaw. He was a good man of a sober disposition. He had been my psychiatrist for more than a year and a half.

The dung beetle, which lives in the deserts of Africa, makes small balls of dung, lays eggs in them and buries them underground. It takes care of them till they hatch. I'm reading about insects in a thick encyclopaedia and grieving over the state of humanity. I sometimes dream I've turned into a dung beetle foetus buried underground and that I'm now inside an egg. I imagine that the pain is a giant, warm-hearted beetle that has become my mother.

This morning, along with the pizza adverts and the free newspapers that come through the letter box, I received a letter from the hospital. A fine of 27 euros because I missed an appointment with the new doctor two weeks ago. Well, do I deserve such punishment? After that, something else bugged me: I realised it has been ten years since I picked up the telephone to ask after my mother and brothers, when I know very well what hell they're going through. Other bugs of every shape and form trap the air in my head.

The man began to examine his chunky heart from every angle, and ask why from an early age he had started wrapping it in a thick layer of cement and iron. He didn't find the answer, just mysterious feelings that didn't help him explain why his heart was so hard and why he was constantly running away from the past. But didn't he want to choose his life for himself and to be his own master? Here he is now, living in a beautiful flat in Helsinki, and in one year little Mariam will go off to school. His wife has savings from her work in the pizza restaurant and is now thinking of opening a restaurant that serves Iraqi dishes. She had given it serious thought: the waitresses would wear a hybrid uniform, combining elements of traditional Iraqi dress with the type of clothing worn by Oriental dancers. The décor would be traditional. If a permit could be secured, a real stuffed camel would stand or kneel in one of the corners. The food would be accompanied by interludes of oriental music. The floor would be covered with carpets with pictures of Sindbad on them. The incense would come out of an old lamp like Aladdin's. She had thought of everything that would play into the fantasies that Finns and Western customers in general would have about the land of *A Thousand and One Nights*. A young Finnish novelist once asked me, with a genuine look of astonishment and curiosity, 'How did you read Kafka? Did you read him in Arabic? How could you discover Kafka that way?' I felt as I were a suspect in a crime and the Finnish novelist was the detective, and that Kafka was a Western treasure that Ali Baba, the Iraqi, had stolen. In the same way, I might have asked, 'Did you read Kafka in Finnish?'

Doctor, we've been monitoring the planet DULL WINTER EARTH for several centuries and we've established that there's no one there but the six beings that the space observation cameras have detected. What's striking is that the six haven't left the confines of their village on the banks of the red river. This is, in fact, a frozen river but we still don't know what it's made of. It looks to us like a river of frozen blood. And from the results of our observations, it seems that one of the six beings is the leader of the group. His house is set apart on the bluff and is shaped like a cup, while the other houses are glass rooms like water bubbles. The houses are close together on a curved line. For years, all we've observed of their way of life is the strict routine they perform every day. The five stay at home all the time, while the sixth sits motionless on the edge of the red river. Then the five come out together and head towards the sixth. They surround him and present him with something we can't see. When they move away to go back to their rooms, the sixth one goes back to his room too. He stays there some time, then goes out and throws something into the river, then goes back to where he sits. We finally decided to wipe them out with laser beams, and we didn't risk getting in touch with them. I think the time for adventures is over. They belonged to that time that had caused the disappearance of our old Earth. What's laughable is that among us there's an old eccentric astronaut who still writes poetry. As you know, our early forefathers on Earth used to engage in this retarded behaviour. The astronaut would say, 'Those six are God!' Can you imagine! After so many aeons of existence, after mankind has achieved complete immortality in its triumph over death, there are still people who believe in God. The astronaut must be punished and subjected to prolonged psychiatric treatment. He's suffering from the belief disease, which is otherwise extinct in this age of ours – the age of eternal voyaging, the second eternal age that lacks any purpose or direction.

But one beautiful calm night the astronaut left his room to go for a space walk. He put on his suit, jumped into space and began to swim slowly, looking at the distant stars. A while later all the astronaut did was rearrange the letters in the planet's name in his mind and read them as DEATH WILL RETURN.

After this minor linguistic discovery, which some of his colleagues saw as pure hocus pocus, alarm spread among the inhabitants of the galaxy and many conferences were held to look into the possible dangers.

Doctor, that's why the stories had to be rewritten. Because the word death had stirred up sensations again.

I don't want to look on serenely and quietly. I'm tired. I want to scream. I'm like any one of you, a mass of schizoid monkeys living in one body. I'm a fish that burns in an oven while it's pouring with rain outside. Yet another image, and yet more poisons pouring out of my mouth. Smile, Mother, so that the dates ripen. Good, I thought the world was just a coded dream and that I was a symbol hunter who needs a hunting net and a laboratory. The books tricked me before the encyclopaedia of human insects could trick me. And finally the dream for which I had wrecked my life collapsed. I now have two wrecks: my life and the dream. I love you, Mother, and I pray that God will stop tormenting you with vulgar black sadness and that the country will be ruled by an angel with a beautiful bottom. Before he set fire to the children's bus, the doctor was treating my depression some of the time, and at other times my aggressive and trouble-making mentality. I can't sleep, Mother. They want to force me to sleep. And you, my brothers, I tell you I'm one of those terrified patients, one of those Kafkaesque mice, a breed that's chased forever. We eat fast and in fear, we sleep with eyes half-closed. The characters in our nightmares are evil cats and barbed wire traps. By the way, this disease isn't contagious, but genetic. Before Kafka appeared they used to call our ancestors the sources of evil. They sent them to the temples to exorcise the demons from their heads. As for now, how can we describe our wretched political life?

My wife, my friends and the head of the Association for the Defence of the Unfortunate are all praying for me to sleep and to receive my due in life. They're right when they feel they are privileged, because those who sleep are kings who are born by day, quietly and in good health, outside the hospital, and they do not know the screams of childbirth. I envy them this peace of mind and graciousness. As for me, you can label me 'distrustful', as well as 'disreputable', because I can't submit my spirit to daybreak stealthily and without protection. I'm also faithless, and I intend to announce a new battle with the pharmacy. That's why I won't visit the doctor from now on. The trouble is that they stop you drinking alcohol when you're taking their pills – those insecticides they offer you with a broad grin. The nurse also gave me the telephone number of a 'suicide paramedic'. Do you think I'm joking? Haven't you heard of this job? The nurse said, word for word: 'You can call this number if you feel you're about to do something dangerous. They'll come straight away.' I didn't believe it when I heard there was an ambulance specially dedicated to the suicidal. But is it to rescue them, or just to satisfy their curiosity, to witness failed attempts at suicide? And what kind of loser would put his head in the noose and then take his mobile phone out of his pocket and call for an ambulance? Okay, okay, okay, I agree to visit the doctor, but on certain conditions: he has to come up with other answers, not the ones I already know. I want convincing answers about my crisis when I wander round the streets at dawn. I want to ask the doctor about that mysterious religious desire that jolts me at such an ungodly hour in the morning.

Thank you, madam. Give me the phone number of your association. Your eyes are beautiful, and this beautiful flower – I mean the earring – is it a daffodil?

Before the doctor was cut in half and burnt the children with his car, I said to him: 'Doctor, did you know that when I leave the house and the cold air touches my face, I feel this desire? Warm water wells up into my head from unknown springs. I feel lighter and then it's like I've turned into a Buddhist cloud. How can I explain it to you?

Look, there's a seagull snatching a small piece of bread from that group of sparrows and taking it up to the roof of the train station.'

Doctor, I can identify my feeling at that moment as a desire to kiss, to stand in front of the station gate like the people who give out free newspapers and adverts, to stand in the way of people in a hurry and to stop them to kiss their hands, their shoes, their knees, their bags. And if they allowed me to bare their arses for a few minutes, to kiss them too. Excuse me, madam, can I kiss the sleeve of your coat? Please, sir, accept from me this kiss on your necktie. Kisses for free; sad, sincere kisses. And very often, doctor, I don't just want to kiss people, I want to kiss the vestiges they leave on the pavements: kisses for cigarette butts, for a key that an old woman lost, for the beer bottles the drunks left behind last night, for the numbers on discarded receipts; kisses that combine the maternal instinct with lust, as day and night are combined in my head.

Then suddenly, doctor, these desires evaporate completely, as happens when a clear sky is invaded by a gang of fat and insolent clouds. Something like torture occurs as if a brutal jailor were pulling out my fingernails. Doctor, I feel as if my jaw has turned into an animal's jaw and a tail has sprouted out of my arse. Doctor, fear runs riot in my throat, which dries up and seeks out a drop of water at any cost, even at the cost of human dignity. Thirst and hatred are mixed up in my head, which turns into a trumpet playing sadistic anthems. So now, all of a sudden, I want to take back those free kisses of mine. I want to cut the balls off that man in a hurry who lights his cigarette at the station gate. I want to dig my nails into the face of that child whose mother is pushing him towards the station. A child to whom they're teaching travel and fear. Another child, doctor. Another sleepless hiatus between night and day.

Doctor, I was born in Baghdad. My grandfather was a peasant farmer who moved to the city. My grandfather thought the streets were like the waterways in the southern marshes. A car hit him and he was killed. My father was a soldier until he passed away from a stroke.

My mother couldn't read or write. My mother mourned in war and in peacetime. I was sitting one midday in July reading Badr Shakir al-Sayyab's Rain Song. *My brothers had become policemen, jailors and people who pray. So by the rules of authenticity I should write a realistic novel about the life of water, about lamentation and the grandchildren of Ali ibn Abi Talib. I should devote my time to studying tradition in order to understand the endeavours of the lice that make my scalp itch. My grandfather came to the city to carry a picture of the leader. My grandfather who ran away from hunger and mosquitoes.*

Doctor, you know there are two types of poison – natural and synthetic – and they are classified according to where they come from or their chemical properties. There are caustic poisons, inflammatory poisons, neural poisons and haematic poisons. The caustic ones damage the tissues directly, the inflammatory ones burn the mucous membranes, and the haematic ones prevent oxygen reaching the blood. I also know that poisons usually reach the body through ingestion, inhalation, stings or sucking. Oleander, jequirity, castor beans, datura, colchicum and hemlock are examples of poisonous plants. Venomous stings and bites are the speciality of scorpions, snakes, stinging fish, and salamanders. The most important symptoms of poisoning, which differ according to how long the poison stays in the body, include the emission of breath with a smell that resembles that of alcohol. You know best, doctor, but let me finish speaking. I was born with this defect – my breath has smelled since I was a child, and the smell is this rotten, vicious tongue. The other symptoms my life has brought me are: dilation and contraction of the pupils, a burning in the throat, nausea, vomiting, diarrhoea, convulsions, delirium, cyanosis of the skin, a defect in feelings of love, fainting or narcolepsy, as well as drowsiness. If someone is poisoned with medicine, you can grill an apple and give it to the victim while he gets to hospital. But cider vinegar is used as an antidote in cases of poisoning with rotten fish or salted mullet or tinned sardines. It is drunk after the stomach has been evacuated through vomiting. There's no need to panic over bee stings or mosquito bites. We take out the sting and rub the spot with garlic, leek leaves or basil. As for when one human stings another, fellow human, it's definitely an unfortunate end and we console the victim at the point of death. By that stage not much is needed, just to light a small candle to drive away the demons that might try to tear at the body of the dead, or to blow quickly into the mouth of the dying person, which helps him in those moments to uncover the vast accumulation of delusions by which he lived.

Doctor, I sit in the cafe for hours and hours until my arse hurts. The young woman who was leaning over her papers and writing has gone out to smoke a cigarette in the doorway. Her pen fell when she stood up. I fell in love with the pen, a pure, honest love for a pen lying angry next to the table leg. The pen of a beautiful young woman who's gone to smoke a cigarette lies there alone, hating its short life. Every movement, doctor, every gesture, however simple or insignificant, gives me the love headache. So I try to look instinctively spiteful. But what does that mean? I don't know. As you can see, I behave like an alcoholic for whom alcohol no longer holds any pleasure. Didn't you notice? I'm embarrassed by the idea of these little love stories of mine leaking out to others. Once I told a friend that I thought about the shirt buttons of someone sitting in the cafe more than I did about the country's wars. I wasn't pretending to be poetic or mad. But the way he looked at me was like an insult.

Doctor, I'm sure you haven't heard the story of the poisoned fish. Do you think I'm some madman talking to you about poisons for no reason? In the beginning of the siege years, in 1991, the story of the father and the fish spread across the country. He had bought a large fish, with some vegetables and some pickles. He grilled the fish himself and prepared the salads. Then he ate with his six daughters with tearful eyes and a troubled heart. Of course his daughters didn't know that he had poisoned the fish. The man couldn't see any other way to prevent his daughters from turning to prostitution. He sold plastic bags in the market and what he earned wasn't enough to live on. He died in the certainty that his wife, who was buried in the Najaf cemetery, would understand. Many people didn't want to call that a crime. But I was thinking about daydreams – the dreams of the man's daughters as they ate their father's delicious fish. I don't know if other people have daydreams when they eat in silence. I know there's no fixed time for such reveries. That's what makes them different from ordinary dreams, which are part of a system, though not a democratic one. It's one of the distinctions of the Daydream Republic. The story of the man was a warning that alarmed people in the early years of the siege. The fish tail on which flies gathered in the rubbish bin wasn't poisoned. A fat cat took it and fed it to her kittens on the roof of the man's house. How I wish there could really be such a cat. Any tragedy that isn't permeated with details invented in an exaggerated and lachrymose way doesn't deserve to appear in the great tragic theatre. Now do you understand what I mean, doctor? The fish tail is another comma. There's a bony comma in my head that prevents me from sleeping. You're right. It's your turn to talk now, doctor. At the time, people didn't talk about the kind of poison in the fish. Instead they talked at length about hunger and the honour of their daughters.

Doctor, you want to say that the world can be as white as your shirt. Okay, doctor. And that man is a comma between the words 'birth' and 'death'. But on the honour of your humanitarian profession, doctor, promise to tell me what this empty blank sentence means, and whether the comma is actually necessary.

Doctor, another comma please. Let me go to the bathroom. When I come back, doctor, I'll tell you about another comma called loneliness. But now let me empty my bowels. I feel as if I've drunk a barrel of mud.

Doctor, did you know there are types of mice that start gnawing their tails whenever they get hungry? And the most important mouse I know, which has helped me predict my destiny, is Kafka's mouse. Have you read it in Finnish, doctor? How can I translate it for you? It's one of Kafka's short poisons and its title is 'A Short Story':

> *The mouse said, 'Alas, the world gets smaller every day. It used to be so big that I was frightened. I would run and run and I was pleased when I finally saw the walls appear on the horizon in every direction, but these long walls run fast to meet each other, and here I am at the end of the room and in front of me I can see a trap that I must run into.'*
>
> *'You only have to change direction,' said the cat, and tore the mouse up.*

Thank you, doctor.

Now, doctor, please get me out of this dung ball. Please.

A Thousand and One Knives

1

AT NOON JAAFAR the referee was waiting at the end of the lane, his army binoculars round his neck and a football in his lap. The boys arrived one after another and surrounded him, joking with him and talking excitedly about the striker in the Sector 32 team. Jaafar reassured them. 'We have Allawi al-Saba. He's the Messi of Sector 29,' he said.

The boys took turns pushing Jaafar's wheelchair. One of them said, 'The Sector 32 team might bring a referee of their own.'

Jaafar wasn't bothered. He told them he knew how to handle that. They reached the field, Jaafar threw the ball and the boys ran after it.

Jaafar was forty-five years old but he was still young at heart. With his passion for sport, his dynamism and his determination, he amazed his friends and his few enemies. He had been the most famous snooker player in Sector 29 and when he was an army deserter the military police couldn't catch him. He was like a fox, but his addiction to snooker halls was his downfall. One evening the military police surrounded him at the Khorasan snooker hall in Karada, where he used to take on the most famous players in the area. They sent him off to the Kuwait War and when he came back both his legs had been amputated. Jaafar was a good lad, one of the boys – that's how the people of the sector saw him. But some of them found fault with his passion for football and the way he hung out with the local youth at his age. Jaafar didn't take much notice of such talk, because the young had to learn the basics of the game. He would organise matches for them and act as referee. He would remind his critics of the famous national squad player who came from Sector 29 and who he claimed to have trained, adding each time: 'A miracle that will save the whole country will be my doing, too!'

On the edge of the football field there was a large rubbish skip that gave off white smoke with a putrid stench that drifted over the pitch. Women, some in abayas and some without, came out of the houses around the field with bags of rubbish. Jaafar watched them through his binoculars while the boys ran after the ball, shouting. With his binoculars Jaafar also watched the boys playing. The Sector 32 team arrived accompanied by a young man with a beard and he and Jaafar agreed that Jaafar would referee the first half and the other man the second half. The match began. Jaafar pushed his wheelchair up and down the pitch at high speed in a frenzied passion. He shouted at the boys, either to encourage them or reprimand them, and when they were too far off he would follow them with his binoculars. 'Goooooooooaaaaaal,' shouted Jaafar. The Sector 32 referee objected that Jaafar was supporting his own team and wasn't impartial. Jaafar ignored his objections. He worried about his players as if they were his own children, and when they fell down he would check their knees and legs for any damage. Sometimes his mind would wander and for a few moments he would see them as ghosts in battle and recall the boom of artillery on the front. But then he would go back to the match and blow his whistle to award a penalty kick, as cheerful and enthusiastic as ever. He dripped with sweat as he pushed the wheelchair around with all his strength to keep up with the boys running after the ball like antelopes.

Jaafar blew the whistle. 'Foul!'

'I swear it wasn't a foul, Jaafar,' objected one of the boys.

'I tell you it's a foul. Don't argue, you idiot.'

'But Jaafar, you were far away.'

'What are these then? Do you think I'm blind?' said Jaafar, holding up his binoculars.

The match ended in a 2-2 draw and the boys pushed Jaafar's wheelchair to the coffee shop. He said goodbye to them and advised them to prepare for next week's match with the Sector 52 team.

Jaafar played dominoes in the Shaab coffee shop and gave the others his analysis of the quality of the various Spanish clubs. His laugh echoed through the cafe and shook the big picture of the imam Ali hanging on the wall. The coffee shop owner said the Americans were going to search the sector that night looking for weapons.

'What does that bunch of cowboys want? It's because of them I lost my legs in the Kuwait War. What do they want next? Fuck them. One day America's going to go to shit,' Jaafar said indignantly, then changed the subject back to football. He and the Real Madrid supporters started arguing and joking. Jaafar was an avid supporter of Barcelona and sometimes Liverpool.

I was waiting for him at the coffee shop door. He came out laughing loudly and gave me a friendly punch in the guts. I pushed his wheelchair and we crossed the street. He asked after his sister, who is my wife, and I said, 'She's well.'

'Are you going to do the disappearing knife trick today?' he asked, coughing. He was a chronic smoker.

'No, but I may talk a little about the interpretation of dreams.'

I knocked on the door and Souad opened it. 'Ah, both of you,' she said as she kissed Jaafar on the head. She helped me get his wheelchair through the narrow doorway. I pinched her bottom and she slapped my hand discreetly, but Jaafar didn't notice.

In the room there was a bare wooden bench and Salih the butcher was sitting on it. Allawi was sitting cross-legged on the ground with a set of green prayer beads in his hand – the same way he sat when he was making a knife disappear.

Jaafar shook Salih's hand and said, 'Hey, Allawi, come and sit on the bench.'

Allawi answered proudly, 'I've never sat on a chair or a bench.'

'You mean in all your life?'

'Of course.'

'But you're only fifteen, damn it. Anyone who heard you would say you were as old as the dinosaurs.'

Jaafar laughed his booming laugh as he adjusted the photograph of his father on the wall.

Souad disappeared into the kitchen and I sat next to the butcher. Jaafar turned his wheelchair to face us. Souad came back with a tray of tea, sat on the carpet close to Allawi and poured the tea, smiling amiably at everyone and winking at me several times. I blew her a kiss. Jaafar turned to me and said, 'Hey, love birds, we've got work to do. When the meeting's over you can throw each other as many kisses as you want.'

In his weird woman's voice, the butcher said, 'Now, Jaafar. Anyone who heard you would say this was a meeting of some underground party that was going to change the world. We've made so many knives disappear, and Souad always brings them back again... And it's been going on like this for ten years.'

Allawi laughed and said, 'I've been making knives disappear all my life. But I want to go on making them disappear again and again and I don't know why.' Jaafar changed the subject and asked Allawi whether Umm Ibtisam would be coming today. He replied that he was certain this time, because she had sworn to him three times by Ali's son Abbas that she would come. 'She must be on her way now. You know the shitty Americans have closed half the roads.'

2

We were like one family. Our knife-handling skills weren't the only thing we had in common. We also shared our problems in life, our joys and our ignorance. We were buffeted by all forms of misfortune and several times we grew disappointed with the knives. There were other concerns in life. We almost split up on several occasions but we were drawn back together by the strangeness and pleasure of our gift, by the feeling among all of us - except, perhaps, Salih the butcher - that knives could be a solace and give our lives the thrill of uncertainty.

Ten years have passed since we became a team in the knife trick. Allawi joined us three years ago. I continued my studies and went to the Faculty of Education. Souad went into the sixth year of secondary school, specializing in sciences, and dreamed of going to the Faculty of Medicine. Salih the butcher has extended his shop, divorced the mother of his children and married a young woman who had a bad reputation in the neighbourhood. Jaafar found Allawi a job in the factory that makes women's shoes. He didn't want Allawi to stay in the market playing with knives. Jaafar himself was the same as always – busy with football, refereeing, dominoes, the coffee shop, always anxious to ensure that our group didn't fall apart and constantly seeking out new talent in football and also in the knife trick. He believed that our knife skills were a secret vocation that would change the world. As to how and why and when, these were all unanswered questions but he had nothing to do with them. 'I've never even read a newspaper in my life. How could I understand the secret of the knives?' he said.

The butcher, Allawi, Jaafar and I had the ability to make knives disappear. Souad was the only person who could make them reappear but she couldn't make them disappear. Souad's difference compounded the mystery of our talents, which did not progress one step despite the passage of all those years.

Two years ago I was assigned to read books in order to

find out what the knives meant, and I soon came to the idea that the knives were just a metaphor for all the terror, the killing and the brutality in the country. It's a realistic phenomenon that is unfamiliar, an extraordinary game that has no value, because it is hemmed in by definite laws.

I married Souad a year and a half ago. It was Jaafar who arranged this early marriage with my father. Souad's cousin had approached Jaafar with a proposal to marry her. Jaafar didn't want Souad to move away from us and go to live in the village. He wasn't unaware of the tentative affection we felt for each other. My father was persuaded straight away, especially as Jaafar made my father an attractive offer. He said he would buy Souad and me a small house. My father agreed at once because he wanted to relieve the strain in his own house. We were nine brothers and three sisters all living in two rooms and my father was struggling to keep the family afloat. He worked as a baker and my mother gave injections to sick people in the neighbourhood, though she didn't have a nursing certificate. In fact she was illiterate and because she was so kind, people called her the angel of mercy.

When I was a youngster I played on Jaafar's football team. He discovered my talent by chance. He was watching me as I made a knife that some boy was holding disappear. He was ecstatic and started to hug me. He cheerfully took me to their house and introduced me to young Souad, whose eyes projected the force of life like a strong and beautiful flower. The next day Jaafar took me to Salih the butcher's shop and introduced me to him.

In those days we used to meet in Jaafar's house, but his mother and his five brothers would disturb us so then we moved to Salih's house. He had a room on the roof of the house where he raised birds. We would put the knives on top of a round wooden table and make them disappear one by one, then Souad would make them reappear. We would exchange views and try to analyse the trick. But the conversation soon moved away from knives and turned to jokes and stories about the people in the sector. We continued to meet in the pigeon loft until I got married and Jaafar bought us that small house. Jaafar had considerable wealth from a business he'd been in since he was young. He used to deal in pornographic magazines that were banned, but he was careful to cover his tracks, selling them only in wealthy neighbourhoods.

It was I who discovered Allawi and brought him into the group. I was in the street market buying rat poison when I saw a group of children and adults in a corner of the market, gathered in a circle full of curiosity. Allawi was sitting cross-legged as usual, with a number of small knives of various types next to him. He didn't make knives disappear for free. People would give him a packet of cigarettes or enough money for a sandwich or to buy a grape juice or pomegranate juice, and as soon as he felt it was worth his while he would throw one of the knives onto the ground in front of the spectators and ask them to touch it to make sure it was a real knife. Then he would ask them to stand back in a slightly larger circle so that he could breathe and concentrate. Allawi stared at the knife for thirty seconds, as we all did, and as soon as tears started to glisten in his eyes the knife would disappear. The audience would applaud in amazement and admiration, and Allawi would then wait for the spectators to come up with enough money for him to repeat the trick with another knife. His main problem was that he depended on stealing knives to replace the ones he made disappear. That put him in many tricky situations.

The tears and the thirty seconds were the common denominator between us all when it came to making knives disappear and reappear. As I said, were it not for Souad the knives would have disappeared for ever and we would all have been like Allawi before he joined us – just a knife thief. Salih the butcher faced the same problem before he met Jaafar and Souad. Salih loved the trick: in his shop he would stare at knives at length until they disappeared. But after the trick he had to buy new knives. Allawi made money in the market from his gift while Salih would lose out. If it wasn't for Souad, he said, he would have died of hunger. Every day Souad brought back the knives he had made disappear, and we were sure this was the only reason the butcher stayed with us all those years.

We were constantly on the lookout for a new member of the group with powers like those of Souad. We would meet every Thursday and make a set of knives disappear and Souad would make them reappear in the same way: tears and a few seconds!

I could make knives disappear easily. I began by making my mother's knives disappear in the kitchen when I was a child. In the beginning my mother would almost go crazy, but when she discovered my secret she and my father took me to a cleric to consult him on the subject. The man with the turban told them in all confidence: 'Your son is in league with the djinn.' He advised my father and mother to pray and wash the courtyard of the house twice – once at dawn and again at sunset. When I got interested in football and met Jaafar I stopped making knives disappear at home or at the homes of friends and relatives.

The knife trick didn't have a particular purpose. Maybe Salih the butcher saw his gift as a disease and as far as he was concerned Souad was the only cure. The feelings and ideas that Souad, Jaafar, Allawi and I had were different to some extent. Jaafar thought it was a secret and sacred vocation and believed that what we did, despite the absurdity of it, was a source of great pleasure, especially as he saw himself as the spiritual father and the leader of the group.

Allawi was addicted to the game. It was like a drug that erased his memory of the painful loss of both his parents at an early age. His father had been a drunkard who argued with the neighbours and who killed a man with his pistol. Before the police arrived one of the dead man's sons, who had seen his father drowning in blood, came to the door of Allawi's father's house with a Kalashnikov in his hand. Allawi's father was standing behind the closed door with the pistol in his hand and his mother was trying to stop him going out. The son emptied a whole magazine of bullets into the door. The door fell in and Allawi's mother and father were killed.

Knives were my pastime and part of my life. Seeking the mystery of the game, I felt like someone looking for a single rare flower on a high mountain range. Often it felt like an adventure in a fable. Many a time I felt as though I was doing a spiritual exercise with the knife trick. The reality didn't interest me as much as the beauty of the mystery attracted me. Maybe this is what drove me to write poetry after I gave up looking for the meaning of the knives.

Illiteracy was one of the obstacles that compounded our failure to understand the trick or even to develop our skills throughout the years. Salih the butcher, Allawi and Jaafar couldn't read or write. It's true that Souad was educated but she practised the knife trick with a childish attitude. She would always remind me, saying: 'Why complicate things, my love? Life is short and we are alive. Treat the knives as a game to entertain us and leave it at that.' Souad repeatedly suggested we open a little theatre in the neighbourhood to amuse the local people by making knives disappear and then reappear, in the hope that this might relieve the gloom of war and the endless killing. But Jaafar was worried about the clerics, because they were acting like militias at the time. I thought he was right to worry; at any moment they could have denounced us as infidels, maybe even accused us of undermining society with alien superstitions imported from abroad. Their superstitions had become the law, and God had become a sword for cutting off people's heads and declaring them infidels.

My ignorance increased when I embarked on the task of researching the knife trick through reading. My education didn't help me much. It was religious books that I first examined to find references to the trick. Most of the houses in our sector and around had a handful of books and other publications, primarily the Quran, the sayings of the Prophet, stories about Heaven and Hell, and texts about prophets and infidels. It's true I found many references to knives in these books but they struck me as just laughable. They only had knives for jihad, for treachery, for torture and terror. Swords and blood. Symbols of desert battles and the battles of the future. Victory banners stamped with the name of God, and knives of war.

After that I moved into works of literature. That was by chance. A single sentence had stirred up a whirlwind of excitement inside me. Then one day, in a café, I came across an article in a local newspaper about a massacre by sectarian fighters in a village south of the capital. They had set fire to the houses of people sleeping at night. The only survivor of the conflagration was a young boy. The boy was purple and in his hand he held a purple rat. They found him asleep in a wheat field. His story went unnoticed in the relentless daily cycle of bloody violence in the country. In the culture section of the newspaper there was an interview with an Iraqi poet in exile who said, 'A closed door: that's the definition of existence.'

The next day I went to Mutanabbi Street, where books are sold. I wasn't a regular visitor. I was terrified by the sight of the stacks of books there, in the bookshop windows, in the stalls in the street and on the wooden carts. Hundreds of titles and covers. I couldn't buy a single book that day. I didn't know what to choose or where to begin. I went back to Mutanabbi Street every Friday and gradually regained my confidence. I started to buy books of poetry, novels and short stories, local and translated. Then our group decided to contribute some money to help me buy more books, in the hope that I would come across the key to the mystery of the knives, and soon the house was full of books. We made shelves in the pigeon loft, the kitchen and even in the bathroom. After a year of voracious reading I was no longer drawn to research into the mystery of the knives, but to the pleasures of knowledge and reading generally. The magic of words was like rain that quenched the thirst in my soul, and for me life became an idea and a dream: the idea was a ball and the dream was two tennis racquets. I didn't understand many of the books on classical philosophy. But enjoyable and interesting intellectual books on dreams, the universe and time began to attract my attention. I felt this created a problem with the group. They would shower me with questions on what I was reading and whether I had come across any clues to the mystery of the knives in my books. I didn't know how to explain things to them. I was like a small animal that had entered the den of an enormous animal. I felt both pleasure and excitement. Perhaps I was lost, and my only compass was my passion and my fear of the diversity of life. One idea invalidated another and one concept disguised another. One theory made another theory more mysterious. One feeling contested another. One book mocked another book. One poem overshadowed another poem. One ladder went up and another went down. Often knowledge struck me as similar to the knife trick: just a mysterious absurdity or merely a pleasant game.

I tried to explain to the group that research into knives through books wasn't easy. It was a complicated process and certain things might take me many more years to understand. On the other hand I didn't want to disappoint the group, especially Jaafar, who was enthusiastic about the books. So I started telling them stories about other extraordinary things that happen in this world and about man's hidden powers. I tried to simplify for them my modest knowledge of parapsychology, dreams and the mysteries of the universe and of nature. I felt that we were getting lost together, further and further, in the labyrinths of this world, without sails and without a compass.

3

Souad opened the door and a stout woman in her fifties, dressed in black, came in. She greeted us shyly. Salih the butcher stood up, made room for her on the bench and stood by the door. Jaafar asked him to sit down but he said he was fine.

Souad asked the woman, Umm Ibtisam, if she would like something to drink.

'Thank you, coffee please,' she said.

Jaafar tried to dispel the woman's sense that she was unwelcome. He started talking about the high price of vegetables, deploring the fact that the country was importing vegetables from neighbouring countries when it had the two great rivers and plenty of fertile land. Then he jumped to the subject of the high price of gas and petrol when we had the largest reserves of black shit in the world. Souad brought Umm Ibtisam the coffee and went back to her place. She sipped the coffee and told Allawi she was in a hurry and had to get back to her children. It was Allawi who had found Umm Ibtisam. He said he was wandering round the old lanes in the centre of Baghdad when he noticed a shop that sold only knives of various shapes and sizes. He went into the shop and started to browse through the knives. A woman in her fifties came up to him and offered to help. He told her he was looking for a small knife he had lost years before, with a handle in the shape of a shark. The woman gave him a puzzled look and said her knife shop was not a lost property office. Allawi pre-empted her, as he put it, by asking if she knew about making knives disappear. She said she didn't know what he meant and offered him a small knife with a snake wrapped around the handle. Allawi examined it and told the woman he knew how to make it disappear. He sat in the middle of the shop and after thirty seconds of concentration and two tears, the knife disappeared. The woman was upset and asked him to leave at once.

Allawi left and went back the next day. He said he only wanted to talk to her but she didn't want to listen. Maliciously and threateningly, Allawi told her that he could make all the knives in the shop disappear at once.

The woman pulled a large meat cleaver off one of the shelves and brandished it in Allawi's face.

'What do you want, you evil boy?' she cried.

'Nothing. Just to talk.'

Allawi sat cross-legged on the floor and asked her if she would like to see another demonstration of making knives disappear. She didn't reply, just stared at him suspiciously and held the cleaver in her hand. Straight off, Allawi started telling her about the gift of making knives disappear and reappear and about our group. This was very stupid of him, because we were wary of talking about the group to outsiders, but Allawi had spent a long time in the market and thought nothing of showing off in front of others.

Allawi said, 'The woman's face turned the colour of tomato when I talked about the knife trick. She sat on a chair in front of me and put the cleaver on her lap. Then she started to weep in anguish.' Then she suddenly stood up, closed the shop door, wiped away her tears and told him the story of the knife shop, after making him promise never to reveal her secret.

The woman had five daughters and her husband had been killed when a car bomb exploded in front of the Ministry of the Interior, cutting his body in half. It was a disaster. The woman had no idea how she could support her daughters. Her grief for her husband broke her heart and disrupted her sleep. She had nightmares in which she saw an enormous man slaughtering her husband with a knife. The nightmare recurred often, and every time the man would slaughter her husband with a different knife. Umm Ibtisam told Allawi she couldn't understand why the knives appeared in her dream.

A month after the nightmares started, Umm Ibtisam came across a knife in the back garden of her house. It was an old knife. She contacted her brother because she was alarmed by its sudden appearance. Her brother started to ask the neighbours about it but they denied it was theirs. The knife aroused his interest. He said it looked like an antique. He calmed his sister down and told her he would ask his oldest son to stay a few nights with her and her daughters. The man came back a week later with a large sum of money, after selling the knife in the antique market. He told her the knife was valuable and dated from the Ottoman period. The brother joked with the woman, saying, 'Let's hope you find other knives and make us really rich.'

Umm Ibtisam said the nightmares then stopped. But in the same place in the garden six knives appeared, in this case kitchen knives. Umm Ibtisam kept the knives and this time she didn't tell her brother. The knives continued to appear and in the end she told him. He didn't tell anyone the secret of the knives because they were waiting to see how long they would continue to appear in the garden. They carried on appearing, but it was rare for an old one to turn up. Once, a knife dating from the Abbasid period turned up and her brother sold it on the black market for a large amount. He told his sister that God was providing a livelihood for her and her daughters because her husband had been killed without good cause. He suggested opening a shop to sell the knives. The brother rented a small shop close to her house, and so Umm Ibtisam started selling knives.

Umm Ibtisam asked Jaafar to swear to keep her secret because this was her livelihood. She added nothing to what she had told Allawi, who had invited her to attend our meeting. Jaafar swore to God and on his honour that he would keep her secret, and invited her to join the group. But she didn't take up the offer, because all she wanted was for us to leave her alone. Souad embraced Umm Ibtisam, with tears in her eyes, perhaps for the strangeness of life's agonies.

Souad took her to the door and handed her a bag full of cake, saying, 'A simple present for the girls.'

None of us said anything. So there were knives appearing in other places. That meant the plot had thickened.

We were all smoking – Jaafar, Salih, Allawi and I, even Souad who had slipped a cigarette out of my packet, although she didn't normally smoke. We noticed the thick cloud of smoke in the room and burst out laughing together. Jaafar began to cough like a decrepit old man. We took out our knives and started to play. I told them about the earliest book on the interpretation of dreams, which appears on a tablet from the Sumerian city of Lagash. The story goes that Gudea, the ruler of Lagash, was praying in the temple when he suddenly fell asleep.

'I'm off to work,' said Salih in his effeminate voice and left.

4

A year after I graduated from the Faculty of Education, Jaafar the referee suddenly disappeared. We didn't leave a hospital or police station unsearched. We contacted people who had ties with some of the armed groups and kidnap gangs. But to no avail. The ground seemed to have swallowed him up, along with thousands of others in the country. Souad was in her second month of pregnancy and had postponed her studies at the Faculty of Medicine. I was very worried about her. She was frustrated and sad, like a bird whose wings have been broken in a storm.

The kids in Sector 29 were also sad that Jaafar had disappeared. They organised a football tournament by themselves for teams from the other sectors and called it the Referee Jaafar Tournament. They sent me an invitation to referee in the final.

The days passed slowly and sadly, like the miserable face of the country. The wars and the violence were like a photocopier churning out copies and we all wore the same face, a face shaped by pain and torment. We fought for every morsel we ate, weighed down by the sadness and the fears generated by the unknown and the known. Our knife trick was no longer a source of pleasure, because time had dispersed those mysterious talents of ours. We had been broken one after the other, like discarded mannequins. Our group had fallen apart. There were no more meetings or discussions. Hatred had crushed our childish fingers, crushed our bones.

It wasn't easy for a recent graduate like me to find work. The religious groups had opened schools that taught children to memorise the Quran. They offered me work in their schools until I could get a government job, so I got involved in teaching children the Quran and gave up the knife business. From time to time I wrote angry, aggressive and meaningless poems.

Allawi moved out of the capital and wandered around the towns in the south. He toured the markets showing off his skill at making knives disappear, but earned a pittance. Then we heard fresh news about him: he had broken into a restaurant and was arrested for stealing knives from the kitchen. He was sent to prison and we heard no more of him. Souad, friendly and loving, continued to visit Salih the butcher to bring his knives back, and in return Salih would give us the best cuts of meat he had.

One winter's morning I was at school teaching the children the Iron Chapter of the Quran when the principal came in and told me that a strange young man wanted to talk to me about something important.

He was a tall man in his mid-twenties, and his name was Hassan. He said he wanted to talk to me about Jaafar the referee. I asked the principal for permission to take a break and went to the nearby cafe with the man. We ordered tea and he told me what had happened to Jaafar:

The security forces had set free some hostages from a terrorist hideout and Hassan was one of the people freed. He said he had met Jaafar in the place where they were holding the hostages, a house on a farm on the outskirts of the capital. They had abducted Jaafar because he was trading in pornographic magazines in a wealthy neighbourhood where policemen lived. Hassan said they had brutally tortured him. The terrorists told Jaafar that God had punished him when his legs were amputated during the war but Jaafar hadn't repented and had gone on selling pictures of obscenities and debauchery. So the terrorists had decided to cut off Jaafar's arms as a lesson to any unbelieving profligate. The terrorists assembled all the hostages to witness the process of amputating Jaafar's arms. They couldn't believe what happened next. Hassan said that whenever the terrorists approached Jaafar, the swords they were holding disappeared and tears were streaming from his eyes. The terrorists didn't have a single sword or knife left. They were terrified of Jaafar and said he was a devil. They stripped him naked in front of us and crucified him against the wall. They hammered nails into the palms of his hands and he started writhing in pain, naked, with no legs. They decided to amputate his arms with bullets. Two men stood in front of him and sprayed bullets into his arms. One of the bullets hit his heart and he died instantly. They dragged his body to the river, collected some dry branches and poured some petrol on. They set fire to him and chanted 'God is Most Great.'

Souad and I had a beautiful boy and we called him Jaafar. I continued working in the religious school. I never managed to tell Souad what had happened to her brother. I suppressed the horror that his death caused, and I loved Souad even more. She was my only hope in life. She went back to the Faculty of Medicine and time began to heal the wounds, slowly and cautiously.

Umm Ibtisam came to see us. Her financial situation had greatly improved. She said we were good people and she hadn't forgotten us. She offered to open a large shop in the neighbourhood for us to sell knives.

Our business was profitable, though sometimes I would unwittingly make one knife or another disappear. At night I would start by kissing Souad's toes, then creep up to her thighs, then to her navel, her breasts, her armpits and neck until I reached her ear, and then I would whisper, 'My love, I need help!'

She would pinch me on the bottom, then climb on top of my chest, strangle me with her hands and say: 'Ha, you wretch, how many knives have you made disappear? I'm not going to get them back until you kiss me a thousand and one times.'

I kissed every pore on her body with passion and reverence as if she were a life that would soon disappear.

When young Jaafar was five years old, his gift emerged: like his mother he could make knives reappear.

About the Author

Hassan Blasim is a poet, filmmaker and short story writer. Born in Baghdad in 1973, he studied at the city's Academy of Cinematic Arts, where two of his films *Gardenia* (screenplay) and *White Clay* (screenplay & director) won the Academy's Festival Award for Best Work in their respective years. In 1998 he left Baghdad for Sulaymaniya (Iraqi Kurdistan), where he continued to make films, including the feature-length drama *Wounded Camera*, under the pseudonym 'Ouazad Osman', fearing for his family back in Baghdad under the Hussein dictatorship. In 2004, he moved to Finland, where he has since made numerous short films and documentaries for Finnish television. His stories have previously been published on www.iraqstory.com and his essays on cinema have featured in *Cinema Booklets* (Emirates Cultural Foundation). After first appearing in English in *Madinah*, his debut collection *The Madman of Freedom Square* was translated by Jonathan Wright and published by Comma a year later (2009).

Madman was longlisted for the Independent Foreign Fiction Prize in 2010, and has since been translated into Finnish, Spanish, Polish and Italian. A heavily edited version of the book was finally published in Arabic in 2012, and was immediately banned in Jordan. Hassan has won the English PEN Writers in Translation award twice, and was recently described by *The Guardian* as 'perhaps the greatest writer of Arabic fiction alive'. This is his second collection.

This book has been selected to receive financial assistance from English PEN's Writers in Translation programme supported by Bloomberg. English PEN exists to promote literature and its understanding, uphold writers' freedoms around the world, campaign against the persecution and imprisonment of writers for stating their views, and promote the friendly co-operation of writers and free exchange of ideas.

Each year, a dedicated committee of professionals selects between 6-8 books that are translated into English from a wide variety of foreign languages. We award grants to UK publishers to help promote, market and champion these titles. Our aim is to celebrate books of outstanding literary quality, which have a clear link to the PEN charter and promote free speech and intercultural understanding.

In 2011, Writers in Translation's outstanding work and contribution to diversity in the UK literary scene was recognised by Arts Council England. English PEN was awarded a threefold increase in funding to develop its support for world writing in translation and, as of April 2012, the programme will also fund translation costs directly.

www.englishpen.org

ALSO AVAILABLE FROM THE SAME AUTHOR:

The Madman of Freedom Square

Hassan Blasim

Translated from the Arabic by Jonathan Wright
978-1905583256

'Perhaps the best writer of Arabic fiction alive...'
– The Guardian

From hostage-video makers in Baghdad, to human trafficking in the forests of Serbia, institutionalised paranoia in the Saddam years, to the nightmares of an exile trying to embrace a new life in Amsterdam... Blasim's stories present an uncompromising view of the West's relationship with Iraq, spanning over twenty years and taking in everything from the Iran-Iraq War through to the Occupation, as well as offering a haunting critique of the post-war refugee experience.

Blending allegory with historical realism, and subverting readers' expectations in an unflinching comedy of the macabre, these stories manage to be both phantasmagoric and shockingly real, light in touch yet steeped in personal nightmare. For all their despair and darkness, though, what lingers more than the haunting images of war, or the insanity of those who would benefit from it, is the spirit of defiance, the indefatigable courage of those few characters keeping faith with what remains of human intelligence. Together these stories represent the first major literary work about the war from an Iraqi perspective.

Longlisted for the 2010 Independent Foreign Fiction Prize

'Blasim pitches everyday horror into something almost gothic... his taste for the surreal can be Gogol-like.' – The Independent

'Crisp and shocking.... Too febrile and macabre to file under reportage, this cruel, funny and unsettling debut has hooks and twists that will lodge in any mind.' – The Guardian

'Blasim moves adeptly between surreal, internalised states of mind and ironic commentary on Islamic extremism and the American invasion... excellent.' – The Metro